If you Change the Words
you Change the MEANING

Copyright© 2009 by Ellen Allen
Cover Design Tony Neustadter

Psalm 23 was taken from the New American Standard Bible

ISBN 0984423362
EAN-13 9780984423361
LCCN 2011930615

If you Change the Words you Change the MEANING

Novel by

Ellen Allen

Your Time Publishing, LLC P.O. Box 872365 New Orleans, Louisiana, 70187

If you Change the Words
you Change the MEANING

Special Thanks and Unconditional Love

"Bobo"
"Irie Girl"
"Miss Laya"
"My Momma"
"FG Man"

For your time, patience, wisdom, and
understanding

Foreword

In writing this book I was a bit skeptical and that's putting it mildly. I was downright scared, because this is a collaboration of several different perspectives not all of them belonging to me. My faith was questioned by some of my dearest friends and close associates, but I knew my work was worthy of a voice. The messages contained within these pages are not for everyone. I say that with the utmost understanding of people's personal opinion. In order for you to truly embrace this mind set, you have to be willing to take your rose-colored glasses off, and feel the spirit and energy that went into each and every word. In all of my writing about human attractions and reactions in association with human emotions, it was hard to capture the truth, so I've searched with unbridled passion for words to share its raw truth. I have labored for years' wanting to write and complete an artistic piece of fiction. Now I have emerged from my fear and can face the world and its critics.

Prior to the devastation of Hurricane Katrina I had worked on a manuscript for three years only to lose it to those mighty flood waters. Once I grasped the magnitude of that disaster, the loss of my manuscript seemed minute; however, I will piece together my thoughts and ideas for a future comeback of that lost treasure.

This writing establishes a pattern that is commonly unspoken of in our communities, along with the acceptance and enabling of inappropriate behaviors in fear of contributing to the isolation, rejection, and the possible death of ourselves or others. At some point, the tough choices in life we are forced to make may seem harsh, but what else are we to do when our lives are turned upside down by the woes and chaos of this world. When there is no specific answer to our pleas, and we have lost ourselves in another person's turmoil, and we are incessantly saturated in this unreasonableness where do we go? Where our morals are compromised by the insanity we fondle, and our hearts are caressed by the secrets we choose to keep. In the life we lead, the people we meet, and the paths we cross there is bound to be at least one character that we see in this novel that reminds us of someone, and hopefully it is not ourselves. No rational human being would ever think there is any correlation to them in this book, listen carefully and let the pages speak to you. It will broaden your understanding, possibly heightening your insight as to how far we have deteriorated in our thought process and rational thinking abilities. Drug addiction is a monster uncontainable by love alone; this problem is not uncommon in today's society. There is a healing of the addict's mind that must take place before true love can be embraced. I hope you enjoy the read.

Chapter 1

This morning I woke up in prayer as I often do, and something exciting happened, my eyes popped open after months of dreading the light of day. I thanked God for the breath of life he allowed me to inhale. With the dawn of a new day I was in love again, delighted with my existence, feeling safe in my own skin, protected in my thoughts and nurtured in his divine wisdom.

I felt loved by the only person that counts, me. I realized that in order for everyone around me to feel loved, nurtured, and protected I must love myself enough to accept change, expect challenges, and embrace choices. People in general attempt to fix the problems they face from their hearts; this is my perspective, but often times it leads to disappointment and frustration in spite of giving it their best shot.

I have found my way amidst all the lies, hurt, and shame. Wisdom is a powerful vessel not reserved entirely for gray-headedness. I am working through my issues with co-dependency and

1

control   all   due   to   the   relationship   I   am
establishing with my higher power.

Know Him

It has been some time now since I went to bed
Waking up without thoughts of him in my head
Settling into the reality I respectfully dread
Finding the moment I am no longer afraid
Of the choice made to abandon the thread
In the sheets we spiritually vowed and made

Sitting with my back up against the wall
Not wanting to walk or crawl
As he pursued the fleshly call
Of vanity causing a pitfall
The oddly shaped off white ball

Slowly rising up holding my lovers hand
Heeding his command
To pray for strength to withstand
Any and all adversity
Against my own inequity
Running from reality
Sitting in abnormality
Fighting invisibility
Lacking honest scrutiny
Of myself in others activity
Blinded by their audacity
To submerge me in
Bullshit!

Here I am wobbling but steady as I go
Making conscious decisions to let things flow

Into my masters hand
He devised the plan
To help me stand
And
Now I shall follow un-reluctantly
In regaining my righteous sanity

Chapter 2

By the time I met Able his addiction was established, but like in most young relationships it remained hidden, ours was no exception. All I knew was the young man I met two years my senior had a swift walk and a beautiful smile; *My oh my he was a good looker*. He said and did all the things a girl like me, quiet and unassuming, would never have expected from such a fine young man. I thought I was the only one, not knowing whatever the pickup line was, had been used a thousand times before. He was extremely generous, free spirited, a touchy-feely kind of guy, now that I think back maybe I was the one instigating the intimate touching. It seemed easy for him to operate amidst all his pain because he was street smart and quick, still is.

The love between Able and I was a love like no other, one that I had never experienced before, who would have guessed that it wouldn't last a lifetime. He was a man of exquisite integrity, strength unleashed, but a paragon of confusion that lay beneath the skin of this man I loved. I loved him before I understood his past and pitied his present all the while fearing his future. His name is Able his heart is Cain and his soul is doomed.

When we met he was a young man, reentering society for the first time. This was September 29, 1985 after he had spent his fifteenth and sixteenth birthday in a rite to passage program, where he was supposed to learn how to be self-sufficient. On October 1, 1985, after his release he began a new journey that would turn into our twenty-five year love affair. Able was introduced to the drugs by a few of his loving family members and home boys. This was the start of his lifelong struggle with drug addiction.

After eighteen months of secretly courting, Able and I knew we would be together for the rest of our lives. He touched me in ways that I had never known; he took his time sliding his hands naturally over my curves. With this being both of our first time we shied away from complete nudity as he draped my overly matured body in the sheets and began to rub his hands gently up my inner thighs. In comparison to my peers, I was brick house fine especially for a girl my age. It made me uncomfortable when grown men would howl and whistle as I walked by. After Able and I took our relationship to the next level, I understood why they howled. In Able's arms I felt comfortable and safe.

My mother would never approve of me dating; especially a guy from Newburg high-rise; Able would be a misfit in my circle just as I was a misfit in his. After our first time, we became inseparable. I wanted to be with him all the time, which was impossible, because I was attempting to complete my last year of high school. He was about education, having graduated two years earlier from John McDonough with full honors. I remember trying to ditch class to go see him. The very first time I showed up at his apartment he turned me around, marched me back to school, scolding me like a parent. I can hear his exact words, *baby girl not even love is worth sacrificing your education, we have all the time in this world to do that thing we love to do,* that's the Able I knew even through his addiction.

He was unaware of the changing times, of how drugs were being changed by people who wanted to have lifelong customers, and the debilitating effects of crack cocaine, and how it would affect his life in the long run. At that pivotal moment, Able needed a goal and the love and support required to reach his dream, instead he was offered a glass pipe and a little white ball as his right to passage into adulthood.

Able's dream was to add purpose and meaning to his life, he longed for a better life than the one he had experienced thus far. However, no one informed him that smoking crack was highly addictive and mind altering, a drug that would enslave his dream.

I've heard that once you use this particular drug it's like a piece of red clothing mistakenly getting thrown in with the white clothes and regardless of how much you wash them the whites never regain their brilliance. It is scary to think one drug could be that powerful, a magnetic force, robbing a person of their illumination. What I find startling is that anyone professing to love another person would introduce them to something as harmful as crack. I guess their misery was not limited to self-inflicted abuse.

My mother's love contributed to my growth enabling me to blossom into a beautiful young woman. I remember growing up with an abundance of love, affection, and admiration being showered upon me; not one family member or friend ever considered opening my mind up to the injustices of addiction. There are those skeptics who would say don't waste your time on a dope fiend, junkie, crack head or whatever name people give to it. They say they're not worth your energy but those people don't know my Able, they only see my Cain and the worst thing about that is they don't care whether he lives or die.

I know nothing of abuse or the feeling of loneliness that permeate the lungs of drug addicts. I watch others around him pursue a course opposing his ability to breathe and I am stunned at their relentless attacks to keep him fogged in addiction. They will do anything to see him down and out even if it means death. He is my Able, he is my Cain, and I refuse to allow room for his destruction at the hands of others.

Familiar ties derive pleasure from plotting and planning their next move in mounting up against us. I, however, see the benefit of those haters stepping aside, to give Able and me an opportunity to live a peaceful life. I have always fought for what is mine, claiming victory more often than not. My battles are won in words and deeds unlike Able's family who get some sort of brutal thrill out of taking things to the street and coming to physical blows. Watching my friend follow a path of destruction for many years was painful enough. Once we added to our friendship the component of intimacy, it only fueled my desire to save my lover from the constant negative influence of his family, friends, and drugs.

These people often applied pressure by means of superficial tactics, leading him to believe his opinion counted for something, but the discussions always took place when he was there for a party, a funeral, or a wedding where drugs were available. The gatherings they had always turned into block parties where everyone and anyone were invited. By night's end, the police would be called out to end the inevitable altercation, which was fueled by the drinking and smoking or other illegal substance abuse.

Able's desire to belong will always come at great cost because he keeps searching for that bloodline love that controls his heart strings. He needs mans' approval and fears being isolated from his family. Able feels that if he doesn't attend a family function they will think that he is being high and mighty but they don't understand that he's trying to stay clean and sober. He never takes me to these affairs because he doesn't want me exposed to their lifestyle, *yeah right*, the real reason is that he knows I won't attend, because of their lifestyle. He shouldn't attend either but who am I to tell a grown man where he can and cannot go. All I can do is suggest maybe another time or another function that is more appropriate for the entire family to attend. It was obvious to everyone that Able's family means everything to him, their time, attention, and love is what he longed for. They are all aware of his susceptibleness to relapse, so you think they would consider having a picnic where no illegal drugs are being used, distributed or given away like candy, but they won't, not even for the sake of their brother.

Don't let me even mention the Sunday dinners, and family gatherings I have hosted where they bring their trifling behaviors and expect me to conform. They must have had me confused with Able's previous girlfriends. I know how to ask fools to leave if need be; force them from my presence, because I will not be forced into acceptance of contemptible behaviors. One thing I

9

don't understand is his choice to actively pursue
acceptance , ultimately falls back on him, we are
no longer dealing with a young impressionable boy,
Able is capable of making rational decisions that
will affect his future. I know that his strength
far surpasses his demons if he only knew and
believed in his own power.

One of the things Able has to do is fest up
to the hollow darkness that lingers in the back of
his mind by letting go of the past. Loving this
man, with a past plagued in setbacks, a present
haunted in conflict, and a future reserved for a
horse drawn carriage, I find this to be the
hardest reality I can imagine. The depth of the
mighty Mississippi's water has no bearing on the
compassion I feel for my lowly Cain. I believe in
my heart that my Able will be strong again;
displaying that fierce courage that has been his
trademark for more than two decades. What others
do not see is his inner person; whose name is
determination, Able is a fierce go-getter, leaving
no room for error when he is focused on doing the
right thing. For as long as I have known Able, and
pitied Cain I never understood his conflict until
now, it all goes back to years unknown and
unfiltered with speculation.

Chapter 3

There are many people in Able's family who have lived and experienced the same things as my Cain and not one of them sees the story of their lives quite the same. At some point, I would think you could get a least two of these people to verify a story, but not here. Their lives and stories all differ greatly; however, one thing is evident all of his siblings seem tormented by the one fact that I am privy to know, and that is that they all grew up motherless. Growing up without the love and support of their own mother meant they needed more of God's grace to get by. Her presence may have made a world of difference, but because Able didn't have a mother he lingered in discontent. From what I have gathered, Able was born into a family, the third child, he and his older sister shared parents. The siblings to follow each had their own fathers to figure out. Through no fault of her own my Able's mother fell ill when he needed her most. These may or may not be true stories but this appears to be one of those areas that no one seems to have a clear picture of. Some say she suffered from epilepsy, others say she was beaten by a disgruntled lover,

11

yet still others claim a jealous girlfriend had slipped her a *mickey,* whichever incident it was, it still causes Able to cringe and tears to well up in his eyes with the mention of her name. He wouldn't talk about his loss unless he was depressed; even then it's more of a gnawing at his heart than a verbal choke. It's easy for me to say purge your emotions because I was fortunate to have my mother. Able was shackled to his pain in ignorance not realizing that communicating his hurt would open the door to healing his systematic organ failure.

There is a multitude of gray questionable areas in this family. From the tender age of four, my baby needed his mother and she was unable to care for him and no one else seemed to care much, not one adult relative came forward for the love of an innocent child. At that time, just as today it was all about the Benjamin's. There were ten children who needed to be loved, nurtured, and supported. Everyone boasted about opening their hearts but their hands and feet out ran their generosity to access the government funds they expected to come along with their daughter/sisters children. When they realized that those funds were not what they expected, the children including Able witnessed with their own eyes how quickly family members retracted their offers. As if his mother's illness wasn't enough for a boy his age to comprehend, Able was thrust into different homes and situations. I gathered it could not have been easy just from assessing his current behaviors.

I often wondered if there was any sexual abuse in Able's past. Hinting at the possibility of such abuse would infuriate him. Able would turn up his bottom lip, bulge his cheeks and pout like a little child. I knew that one sided conversation would go no further unless I wanted to talk to

12

myself. I questioned his memory on things of his past, him being young and having to experience so many tragedies before adolescence set in could confuse the immature mind of a child.

The first time Able went to Franklin Towers he was around eight years old, child welfare was called in because someone suspected he was being molested by his uncle's wife. I'm sure something happened but what exactly I don't know. His mother's first cousin mentioned this incident to me one day during a visit; she made me promise not to tell Able. She said that Able had it harder than his siblings because he was one of the middle children who were ignored by everyone but his aunt-in-law. She took a special liking to him and regularly splurged on him by buying him *zoozoos* and *frozen cups*. She thought it was strange, and pulled his uncle aside, and questioned him about it, but he brushed it off calling her an instigator. She knew something wasn't right with the situation but even she let it go.

During the early eighties, incest wasn't something people readily acknowledged took place in their families especially the abuse of a male child by a female predator. Able was removed from that environment for his safety. Of course, at eight years old he wasn't developed enough mentally to understand why it was no longer safe for him there. I guess he had been groomed and then conditioned for that form of acceptance of affections. Maybe that event wasn't as traumatic as growing up without his mother because neither Able nor Cain had ever disclosed that information to me. Come to think about it Able gets very angry at the subject matter of child molesters. The conversation I had with his cousin shed light on some of my unanswered questions; she gave me a little more insight into my husband's past as a child isolated in his pain.

By the time Able reached eight he rarely remembered any expressions of affection and by twelve his encounters with the juvenile justice systems was more like family to him than his kin. Able solemnly remembered crying out for his mother only in vain because he knew she wouldn't be coming. As his thoughts consumed him his hatred grew for those who had institutionalized his mother and discarded his existence, leaving him within the four walls of hell.

Franklin Towers would serve as his home for the next year. Able was removed by social services from the care of his uncle following an investigation into a drug raid at the home where he was being cared for. He remembers the cold dreary nights, the complete darkness when all you could hear were the squirrels running about in the attic. With no one coming to his rescue, Able lost hope in everyone including himself. He wondered why no one seemed to care much. After all Able's father was alive and well, if you consider being an avid drunk and recreational drug user well. He showed no signs to redirect or correct his sons' course of destruction nor was he interested in rearing a child, providing fatherly support, or fostering a functional relationship. Able still to this day harbors resentment toward his father. Even though I've tried to get him to talk to him about his feelings of abandonment it has been cumbersome. Able always said, *it's too late because nothing can change the damaged man I am.* My friend longed for a parent, a confidant, a listening ear, or a meaningful embrace; instead he received cold stares and thoughtless dialogue.

How could a young boy ever gain his self-esteem and self-respect within a system designed to mistreat these troubled youth? I'm not by any means bashing all systems but many are severely dysfunctional. I worked for years in behavior focus groups who had no idea what to do with troubled youth like Able, it's sad that I can speak from firsthand experience, I empathize with him and others like him.

Able speaks despairingly of his encounters in the juvenile justice system and his feelings of the odds being stacked against him from birth. The statistical facts from all over the world show that juvenile justice systems are becoming increasingly entangled in negativity, from the housing situations to employing pedophiles. Until you know these things you are ignorant to the truth. He should be thankful that his encounters didn't end in death. I think his experiences should make him look at the successes in his life.

After Able spent an entire year alone, within the walls of Franklin Tower, he emerged an angry, battered, and bruised boy. Able vowed never to shed another tear for his unfortunate situation, his motherless upbringing, his loveless past and his destructive future. Little did he know that the tears would manifest in more ways than one. The life he would choose to live from adolescence onward would not only cause him to shed tears but scream in agony, for anyone's help, guidance, strength and most of all love.

My poor manipulated Able had been dealt some horrible blows, first with the mental loss of his mother's love, support and guidance, second with the neglect of his father next the sexual abuse of a trusted relative and then foster care.

15

Book Club Notes

Little boy Lost

*It was scary
It was dark
No walk in the park*

*Groping around from sunrise to sunset
While they all place their bet
On the kid with no shoes
And nothing to lose*

*A motherless joke
A fatherless ass
Confused
Misused
Abandoned
Abused*

*I hate the world that
Forgot to protect me,
An innocent child
Turning wild
Skipping in the streets
For my bread and meat
Running about the scorch
Underneath my feet
Racing against time
To avoid my next defeat
No one there to comfort me
Now I am in weigh too deep
Up to my eyeballs in this world's*

Unstable heartbeats
I was only eight
Staying out too late
Swinging on the gate
Hoping that Fate
would
Bring my momma home
So I wouldn't be alone
Oh well that thought is gone
There was no phone
Connecting to his throne

They say he exist but
I never knew him
My eyes are not big enough to see him
My ears have not heard his call
My nose capture not a scent of his presence
My mouth has not uttered a sound to him
My hands have not touched his

I am a
Little Boy Lost

Please teach me!

Chapter 4

ble was arrested, and jailed. I never fully understood that concept, what it meant, what he did; I never personally interacted with or cared that deeply for anyone in trouble with the law. After weeks of trying to understand what was going on, Able had someone call me about his court date. I had never been inside of a courthouse, so even this seemingly normal process was foreign to me. I had no idea what to expect, but I went to support him; all I heard was the judge say that my best friend received a twenty-year sentence. I am thinking for what; I still had no clue as to the prevailing mayhem surrounding crack addiction even if I did, most likely, I wouldn't have understood. What happened is still a mystery to me. I remember being scared, crying, and confused because I didn't want him to go away. The thought of missing Able and the time we spent together, our secret rendezvous' in the courtyard of his apartment complex, the piggyback rides, and our playful games of *catch kiss get a little bit*, was overwhelming. Later I found out he only had two years but it still seemed like an eternity to me. Any time without him was always too long, *still is*.

19

I was trying to successfully complete high school, so being there for his weekly visitation was tiresome; I was falling behind in my school work, sleeping less and less, worrying about Able. I was extremely saddened by his absence.

It was traumatic for me being searched from head to toe as the guards emptied the contents of my purse onto a table, but I never wanted to disappoint Able, even though, he had severely wounded me with his actions, getting locked up when I needed him. He will never understand how frightened I was catching a bus from the upper eastside to the Orleans Parish Prison House of Detention to visit him for thirty measly minutes then leaving with sharp pains whisking my breath away for the next hour or so, until I arrived at the front door of my house.

Able, being my first love meant that I would forever be tied to the myth of once mine always mine. Able was the only male I knew as far as relationships went or should I say what I thought was a relationship. The thought of another man being that close to me never crossed my mind. Now that I'm older I realize neither Able nor I understood what it meant to be in a relationship.

Able would write me the most beautiful love letters expressing his feelings for me, pouring out his heart desires, and I would write back telling him how much he meant to me, and how I needed him. I longed for his touch and dreamed of his lips locked to mine, with his scent lingering in my hair. Mind you, I was still a teenager wanting to do adult things with my sweetie neither one of us knew what the hell we were doing but it felt right at the time. We had experienced our first everything together. I thought in my young mind how did such a nice person get involved in such a bad lifestyle. I was not familiar with his history at this point we only dealt with each other. He hadn't met my mother and I knew none of his family. Able mentioned he had nine siblings, which was the extent of his family ties. I would later meet his entire family.

Those two years brought about many changes, I attended my senior year functions without Able, my best friend, completed high school and started my first job, all because he chose incarceration. His release from jail seemed to reveal a bright future for us. Seemingly, Able was doing well then out of nowhere he was thrown back into jail. I thought what for this time? It was never clear to me why he went to jail the first time, he evidently was on some sort of probation. I am the first to admit that ignorance is my name when it comes to legal lingo, but I found out he violated the terms, and there I was again by myself.

Maybe at this point I should have asked Able what he was going through, but silly me, I never inquired. What was happening with Able, a street savvy woman would have already known the answers to, but this perplexed me, a young woman, barely twenty at the time. Leaving the courtroom for the second time in two years seemed surreal, but for the life of me I couldn't understand why Able was being so unproductive. I walked for a few blocks then found a park bench that looked as empty as I felt; I collapsed into tears as the overwhelming emotions enveloped my body. There I wept bitterly for the reality of his uncommitted heart that was forcing me to see my life without him.

Able and I thought that we would be married with six children, preferably boys, a big house with a double car garage and of course a white picket fence, but as I am a living witness plans change. I knew I would always love him but whether or not we would still be, was a big question mark

21

because I didn't want to become addicted to disappointment.

Able has always believed what he wanted to believe so it came as no surprise that he still to this day refuse to comprehend what his absence did to me. Crying became part of my daily routine; I would read and reread those letters he sent me during his first stint in jail. His dreams, our plans dissipated with every word, we were going to be the family he never had, he was going to be the father he longed for and the only man for me.

Despite growing up in vastly different environments we were planning to establish a powerhouse. Our differences were greater than our infatuation or so called love but that never hindered my determination. Able on the other hand became entangled in sin.

I have always known the trust and love of my mother, the depth of her existence was my fortress. Where was my Able's fortress? Where was his trust? He had none! Granted he had your average family circle grandparents, aunts, uncles, siblings and the like but he had no real foundation, a structure without a secure beginning will collapse eventually. I have wondered why some families make it and others don't, personally, I think each individual contributes to the success or failure with their insight and strength.

Men are capable of ruling the core of their families without uttering a sound, but for some of them they shrink back from headship. Able is so powerful in his spirit that any leadership he brings to the table a confident woman could follow, but with his altering personalities, I can't leave myself open to the tragedies of his mind. His fortress is but a pile of rocks, crumbled and dismantled by his own complicated

insecurities. Able has to make up his mind that
this world will not change him anymore than it
has, and he must move on from his broken past.

Book Club Notes

Chapter 5

The years have passed and there still exists darkness in Cain that can never be erased, a space in time that will never be recaptured and memories that cause his heart to ache. I remember Cain calling some months back begging for my forgiveness. I asked what do you need forgiveness for Cain, he said for letting you go some seventeen years ago. It's four-forty-five in the morning and he's calling with drama. I listened because he was absent his mind, calling, and hanging up before finding the courage to speak. For a solid hour he cried, yelled, screamed, and boast about his many failures and menial successes. I assured him of my love and our friendship suggesting that he should go and get some rest. Cain had been on a binge and once again he denied using but the exhaustion in his voice uncovered his lies.

Able the resister would probably be a more adequate description of this man. Every time problems arose Able would hide behind his work, he said that working around the clock left no time for him to dredge up painful memories of a

25

childhood that went array. I noticed that he would use constant work as a distraction from unsavory behaviors, but working endlessly will not solve his addiction. It's just a temporary fix to impending self-destruction.

The pitch black of night disturbs his sleep. Able grits his teeth, whines and talks, I can never make out what he's doing in his mind but it rattles me enough to awake him from sleep. I ask him what's going on in his head, why is his heart still weighed down with the things he can't change; his silence to my questions is eerily familiar these days. Once his demons direct him to *score* that initial piece of crack, Able goes from being the master of his faith to being conquered.

There was never a time when we wouldn't call or help each other if one or the other was in need. He was my friend, I was okay with whatever, and whoever made him happy as long as he wasn't in addiction, I was satisfied. I must admit however that I remained his friend through his bouts with crack because I no longer felt the need to rescue a drowning man that is what I used to do when we, *were*.

We both had moved on with our lives starting families forging a new level of respectability to our friendship. I had married, become a mother and successful business woman. Able had settled into married life also with his first wife, she was a major dealer of opiates, I thought that the woman he had chose as his partner had his best interest at heart, not knowing her history in the drug trade until I heard on the evening news that she had been shot down, riddled with bullets, DOA.

The night before he married her, he pleaded with me to leave my husband, and if I agreed he would stand her up. I said, *no way!* I never thought he would marry to get even with me but that is exactly what he did. My friend was going to be another woman's husband; this brought back a flood of emotions. Knowing the plans we had and the fact that he declined to be a part of them. Able should have known better but maybe marrying the dealer would be the ideal partnership for Cain.

The early years of his first marriage were unknown to me, unspoken by him, a skeleton in his family's closet. Several years passed before I saw or heard from Able, but I knew he was surviving. Tragedy was Able's sir name, so it was no surprise to me that he deliberately didn't show up for his grandmother's funeral, he could not accept any kind of loss. I'm not certain of his thoughts, but I know he does not do well in handling death.

Shortly after her passing, Cain was on the run from what I heard, and again went to jail, for what only God knows; I would later find out. He was booked and detained for alleged, domestic violence. My Able struggles with substance abuse; fighting women is not his cup of tea. His mother's illness may have been a result of manhandling. This alleged act of domestic abuse changed his life forever and is something I know he would not participate in. Able strongly upholds a belief system of walking away. There is a story behind this arrest that I can recount with almost one-hundred percent accuracy. Cain had been out on a drug binge, his ex-girlfriend probably confronted him, grabbing for a limb, he pulled away from her, she most likely fell igniting her anger, she called the police to say he pushed or shoved her because he would not engage her in a heated confrontation. And this I can vouch for. Unfortunately I have been dragged to the floor as I tried to keep him from the crack that his mind

and body craved. But he never once put his hands
on me.

Chapter 6

When hurricane Katrina hit the Gulf Coast of Mississippi, I evacuated but was worried that he didn't make it out. But at that time I was going through some stuff too. The last I knew for sure he was an inmate, housed downtown, in Orleans Parish Prison, and from the news reports many of the inmates didn't make it because of the water. He was expected to be released from jail late September and be reunited with his family. Even though, a short time before the storm the vine said that Able was doing well I knew he had struggles. To the vine, doing well meant that you were still breathing and not much more. Able had many struggles throughout his life, but the question was not whether or not he could swim, it was his limited opportunity to be set free from the caged surrounding that he was housed in.

I made a tough choice after the devastation of Katrina, which included taking care of me emotionally. I was in a fifteen year marriage that was thick and thin, but never on and off. When we first met, I was on the rebound after Able left me alone. I gave it much consideration then submitted

29

to his request to be his wife. It was good for what my standards of good meant at twenty one. He filled the emptiness that Able left. This man was physically present, giving me the closeness I desired. From the beginning our relationship was rocky, but I held on because I was scared to be without him, not having the affections of a man even if he was a piece of man. His mind was absent but the true commitment was satisfaction enough at that time because our sexual chemistry prevailed.

I grew to love this man giving him my all and everything that defined what a wife was supposed to be, warm, loving, generous, and understanding but I was never appreciated. I believed in the happily ever after scenario, trusting that all wrongs could be made right.

I traveled the world over, from one place to another going when and where I wanted spending as much money as the bank would allow and partied with some of the entertainment industries best. I let nothing stop me. As I reminisce I know that was my escape from reality at times. I was overwhelmed, being a young mother of three stair steps, one in the belly, one in the stroller, and the other barely walking but I did what I had to do. I was able to afford each one of them a comfortable life and we never went without.

I remember once when my ex was unable to work and I had to get some assistance to hold us over until he could return to work. I went in the office of family services for a review of my household's income. The case worker asked all these stupid questions like how much money you have on hand, the names of your children's father, how you pay your bills, how do you buy your personals without income. I couldn't see the value of all those questions; the hassle was not worth the personal invasion so I decided to go get a job. I looked high and low day in and day out for two weeks we had just about depleted our finances when this light bulb came on.

I placed an ad in the newspaper for a girl Friday. I was willing to try my hands at anything, cooking, cleaning, answering phones or walking the dog no task was above or beneath my will to provide for my family. I spent fifteen dollars for my ad to run in Sunday's Times Picayune classified section. About six in the morning my phone started ringing off the hook with prospective clients; I was shocked by the response from that moment on I have made positive strides toward my success. There is nothing I couldn't do to provide for my family. I name my price and make my money. *I know some men who are intimidated by their significant others talents and abilities that is the most insecure part of a man not wanting a strong and confident woman. To me the sexiness of a secure man is enhanced by the strength of his woman.* As I floated thoughts in my head I knew that my change was forthcoming.

The decision to leave my husband wasn't easy, this added to the chaos that was already prevalent in my life. My children had already lost their home, and my husband obviously lost his mind. I needed his support after Katrina. I never once thought about my needs, wants, or desires, before those of my children but this man selfishly whined about his clothes, his music, and his shoes instead of being grateful that he had made it out alive when so many others hadn't. He would leave the children and I for weeks at a time traveling back and forth to his hometown of Tupelo, Mississippi but that wasn't the kicker, every time he made his way back home to us, he had new clothes and shoes, never once bringing me or the children anything. He was a very selfish, materialistic man, deviating between his loyalty to family and his replaceable possessions, cursing the mighty waters of Katrina, in the end his possessions won. When I first met him, I had my doubts about this man because I knew he loved the ladies. If he used drugs, which was a strong possibility, I had neither the time nor energy to see, because I was too busy raising his babies.

Every woman knows when she has reached her limit with the lies and infidelity, and I had arrived at my limit. I was fed up with this relationship, haunted by his indiscretions and the guilt of being naive. Katrina opened my eyes to things I knew existed but had comfortably hidden in the back of my mind. It was time to finally move on so we separated and what a relief. But, by far, it was one of the hardest things I had ever done, telling my children that their parents were no longer going to be together.

The tears that ran down their faces spoke volumes without a sound being uttered. My heart skipped many beats but in that relationship a change had to come.

Chapter 7

After our separation, I made a trip home for the first time since the hurricane and what was left of my home brought me to tears. The walls that were once covered with pictures of my babies were bare, the family trips and videos we made over the years were gone and all I could do was thank God, because that decision to leave made more sense than ever. As I turned to close the front door that was no longer there, I found a piece of paper containing a phone number written with a pencil and underneath it said call me, almost instantly I knew it had to be Able and that he had made it through the storm. Knowing that he wanted to hear from me was comforting but dialing his number was hard because I knew that my marriage was troubled and as in the past, I didn't want Able to become the shoulder I needed to cry on or the ear that I needed to listen to me. I also didn't know what to expect of Able, having survived the storm with his history of intolerance to calamity, I realized pressure and Able could never sit down for a real heart to heart.

I remember vividly how Able always had a way of making me feel as if I was the only girl in the world. I couldn't believe how jittery I was in expectation of our meeting. Seeing one another intensified our bond as time stood still when we were in each other's company. With time and distance between us we had many things to talk about.

Thinking about something other than the problems I was facing with my ex was a relief. So I called Able, and we talked for a while, but seeing him again would have to wait until later because we were miles apart and though I loved talking to him, sitting on the phone for hours was unrealistic.

Able tells me that he had returned home two months before Katrina was on the radar; he decided to wait it out with his girl and their child. Able said all was calm, his work was steady, his family was thriving, and his mind was at rest. He was ready to change his life for the better. He now was a father who wanted to be everything his child needed and more. Able shared many things with me about being an eyewitness to the great conditions that prevailed just moments before the storm. He said that on that bright sunny morning, his life was on track until he heard water rushing, gushing; he was not sure how to describe the tidal waves that were turning the corners of his home. Able said in an instant his life changed just like when he took that first puff of crack. Before he could close the door water pushed him into the foyer and within 4 minutes the house was inundated. He grabbed the baby items and helped his family into the attic. There he sat for two nights until his baby ran out of food, he was compelled to act. Cain surfaced to protect what was his, those in his household and community; this is one time where the conquered and the conqueror manifested for the good, if that's possible. For days people did without their basic needs, some to the point of death, what a tragedy. Able, as well as I, feel that the governments' *Patriotic Act* showed no love for mankind's suffering on August 29, 2005 as it had for the suffering on nine eleven.

The last thing Able needed was more unjustifiable actions to cloud his strong mind. What a senseless crime committed against a community already plagued with poverty, crime, and violence. Don't misunderstand our community the poverty they speak of was always statistical, because the people in our community had an above average mind set, we all knew and still know how to work a nickel ninety-five. Katrina forced Cain out of hiding, the fierceness of Mother Nature, the negligence of human imperfections all contributed to the chaos.

I often speak about making the right decisions; my friends who normally do the right thing for everything did not for Katrina. I always take the cautionary road for potentially dangerous and life-threatening events that involves the lives of my children. What Able/Cain did is what he normally did, survive. One thing I can say with conviction is that Cain is a *good in* when it comes to getting and making his way in the streets. If he lacks anything its belief in himself, because I am well aware of his potential for greatness but my knowing, and his believing are opposite.

During the days immediately following Katrina, Cain was awakened while trying to make sure everyone's needs were met. He did what he had to do, pleading the fifth on most of his ventures. No man or woman could ever be right again after witnessing the horrific sights and hearing dreadful cries of desperation from men, women, and children. I knew from the glimpse of what was shown on television that Able would break, because handling pressure was not, is not his strong suit, especially in relation to desertion and loneliness.

In the days following, Able sent his family on the first available transportation to safety, but after being separated from them for a few weeks, he was eventually reunited with them in upstate New York. Once you experience the sounds of death, there is no way possible to erase the mental pictures generated, and forever they are etched in your memory. In Able's case there was no calm after the storm, things have been an emotional roller coaster ride since, but he still has time to fix them. Katrina offered, Able, a chance to do some real soul searching; he decided to become the man he was supposed to be, at least that's where his heart was. Those boyish ways and unexplained foolishness was going to be a thing of the past.

Four months after our initial phone conversation we reconnected, and met each other for the first time after not seeing each other for years. Able spotted me first, it was not a coincidence either from the first time we met he joked how he could always spot his good thing, living by the motto if his eyes were wired shut he could still picture me, his number one girl. I was sitting on *the bench*, in Audubon Park that we had christened nineteen years earlier, our favorite spot. He crept up from behind, grabbed me with the strong embrace of his arms around my waist and placed a kiss on my cheek. This sent chills throughout my body. We sat for what seemed like a few moments but actually it was hours of interesting conversation about our children and how well they were doing.

Able said he returned to New Orleans, because he was home sick. I said being homesick was a stumbling block for a lot of people. I sympathized, but the reality of Katrina was that the waters would not be reversing themselves, so we needed to make the best lemonade possible. Transitioning myself, I understood many of Able's inner traits, the ones that contributed to us being the people we had become and the genetic makeup that established our roles as mother, father and friend.

I missed the obvious signs of a troubled man but Able had always been a master at hiding his true feelings and this time was no exception. As we talked, I noticed he double talked on issues related to Katrina. It surprised me because he has always been so forthcoming with me. I recognized his glazed over eyes as he recalled the dead bodies of children being carried away by snake and alligator infested waters. Only after several conversations did I realize that Able's failure to disclose or even remember the sequence of events surrounding that awful experience was okay, it was his story to tell not mine. To me that weekend visit was too short because we still had so much to talk about. I hated to let go of his hands. We talked and laughed about everything including our relationships. As I prepared for my journey back east I began to meditate on some of the conversations between Able and I. I worried that he was telling lies by omission. I always notice the things that are unsaid, because those are the important things. They can be life sustaining issues that require immediate attention before they fester and become unmanageable.

Through our entire relation Able always claimed he would never lie to me, had never lied to me. I was uncomfortable feeling as if Able had lied. Immediately I asked him again to clarify some of the statements he made, because the sequence of events seemed unbelievable. Able like most men wouldn't understand the lying by omission accusation. He tried to explain but I soon dropped the issue because it was getting us no further to what actually took place so I did what any good friend would do I listened because it worried him and he had no one to talk to about it.

He still refused to talk about the things that haunted and tormented his soul for all of his adult life. I believe Able's abuse issues stem from something much darker than he is willing to confront. Sexual Abuse! During his childhood Able was shuffled back and forth throughout the juvenile systems. It was about two weeks into our marriage when he said something about me being extremely comfortable with my sexuality; I asked him why he was so uncomfortable with his thoughts and feelings about sex. Able said that he never experienced sexual gratification without pain before. I remember thinking to myself, *Uh, that's it*. He said that I relaxed him; I would expect those sentiments to come from hormones associated with estrogen. The more I probed the more he shut down saying that my questions were something people should never discuss. I told Able if we can't discuss and explore our sexualities together we would have intimacy issues and the issues he had needed to be addressed either with me or a therapist. He arched his eyebrows as if I had violated some code of sexual secrecy. I still had to ask for my own knowledge, had he been assaulted, molested or raped? He asked me if I was crazy, never giving a direct answer. In Able's case, not answering is an admission of some sort of shame or guilt. I let it go but every so often I ask him again hoping for a breakthrough.

This is how Cain reveals himself to me; ignoring questions, hunching his shoulders as if he is a mischievous child, afraid to reveal the truth. As they observe his demons in action, my friend's say that I'm crazy for staying. My first husband was infamous for lying by omission especially when it came down to the ladies. He took me to school on that subject, educating me on the antics of an unfaithful man. Seeing this behavior in Able really caught me off guard.

Able and I have discussed on numerous occasions the benefits of openly addressing the important issues. By running from his past he denies himself a chance to conquer those fears and defeat his enemies. Not a literal fight, rather a mental bout of his will power. In most cases I'm talking to myself, because Able does not see how conjuring up his past will guide him to a better future. Cain refuses to openly admit his chronic illness and the effects of his diseased mind. This only complicates our life together, me trying to direct him towards stability, which he recognizes as important; however, he is afraid of being stabilized. I know it sounds stupid but that's the reality of a drug addict living inside his addiction and me living inside my dependency. My problem is trying to fight for him instead of with him.

Able has to acknowledge the darkness he's groping around in, it's like a light switch that has a short in it and no matter how hard you press, the dimness is evident. When we are alone, just Able and I, we talk, no we communicate and confide in one another our fears, so I don't understand why he doesn't trust me fully. And his persistent omitting or forgetting to answer his phone, pay the bills and most of all the emotional relationship he is maintaining with the mother of his child, has taken me and my emotions to a new level. I find myself doubting his integrity and that scares me. In the twenty five years we've been friends I have never doubted this man's words until now. He has no idea how it effects our relationship, the dark cloud that he has hung over my head, looking into his eyes and feeling devoid of love, longing for the time when I trusted him with my heart and soul. Serving my gut justice, I suspected he was either on cat, crack or crazy possibly all three, but I had no definitive proof. It was however not for lack of questions, he just denied everything, and I just wanted my arrhythmic beats to equalize so I keep silent.

CUFFED

I am spread wide open with my body losing its maiden form-Life
like a consistent hemophiliac bleed causing pain strife

I need you to handle me like the person you want me to be
applying proper pressure without hurting me

The tourniquet if too loose will not save my life
if too tight will cause a struggle-fight

Between my will to live and your subconscious to let me die

If you cannot have me no one else will
living in fear of anyone else experiencing
my touch and my fill
my life linked to my body you desire to kill

Selfish young man you are
not wanting to see your girl move far
measuring the tracks on my tires
smelling the scent of my hair
counting my orgasms is truly unfair
scolding me if it's not enough fanfare

I am already your slave
the one that your mind crave
captured conquered in this man made cave
not knowing how to break free from your venomous rants and rave
afraid to stand up be wise brave

41

Living in secrets, lies, abuse
standing still being knocked down there is no excuse

I am bleeding from the head
lying face down almost dead
from the massive blow even a bully would dread

Looking up into your eyes longingly
for that once outstanding man that used to be
mouth opening with nothing coming out
please save me lord from this last bout

You standing there with my life's fate
all in your hand and there I wait
moaning from the agony I endure as I taste
the end of this journey my whole life but a waste

Chapter 8

I hunger for those months we danced together, sang to each other, and watched the sunrise; it's been too long since we did these things as husband and wife. I miss Able, even in his absence he resides in my thoughts, dwell in my heart and in my prayers. I plead for mercy to be shown on his behalf. Will Able or my life have to end before one of us realizes the toxic nature of this relationship?

Cain has been around for several months now; it's like waking up every day with a fresh perspective, praying, hoping that this day will be the day it gets better but it never comes. I reject the human impulse to give up on my prayers. I know in time that God will answer each one of them, maybe not as I see fit but as he knows will benefit me, so I am not giving up, not yet. We have to pray our way through this addiction but getting Cain away from himself is impossible; I have to devise a plan, but what. Every social setting he finds himself in where God is not alive and active causes a problem for him in the long run; I ask him how often can you play with fire and not get burned? I have seen bigger fish lured and trapped only to be killed. What can I do, because my love is not sufficient to save him from his eventual reality? Able is as stubborn as a bull increasing Cain's continuous denial of the truth about his dark past, and the underlying reason he is using, and abusing crack on a daily basis. This only causes him more pain and sinks him deeper into his depression coupled with his post-traumatic stress he is a ticking time bomb, and his mind can't handle it.

I remember it being a beautiful day last March as we strolled through Audubon Park to celebrate a milestone. Able had gone to his very first recovery meeting. It was a courageous step. I will never forget that date mainly because I remember all the important days in his life. It was the beginning of spring and you could hear the melodious sounds of hummingbirds, feel the cascading breeze moving through the hundred year old oaks and see the sun glaring through the clear blue skies. I was finger feeding Able his favorite chocolate dipped strawberries and mango squares catching the juices with my lips.

It was now four years and seven months after Hurricane Katrina when out of nowhere this young lady frantically ran up to Able, startling me. My mind immediately gravitated towards that show where you are bombarded with lights, camera and accusations of infidelity, but that was not the case, because this young lady knew Able as her hero the one rescuing her from death. She grabbed him holding on to his bearish frame with her petit arms, she spoke volumes with her gestures despite being afflicted in deafness. Able embraced her fighting back emotion himself, his gentle affirmation of her gratitude resonated through my soul. Her name was Jewel, as her mother translated her thoughts, tears rolled down her blushed cheeks, she said, *Jewel thanks you mister for rescuing us from those violent and deadly waters, so many had passed us by, the police, coast guard even the president but you stopped, I will never, ever forget you mister never!*

That was an epiphany, now I knew someone other than myself had glimpsed into Ables' genuine ability to conquer and stand as a strong man. I can't attest to how he felt but I had that same girlish feeling that keeps me in this marriage, the same confidence I clung to, two decades ago. Able would always be my protector and lover regardless of our relationship status. I can't expect others to understand my endless love for Able when I don't understand it myself. Respecting people's choice to stay or go is something that we all can benefit from because we aren't privileged to know the inner workings of those in any relationship.

My friends, people who have known me just as long as Able or longer will tell you, my favorite saying is that a *nigga ain't nothing*, but a man has the power to lift you so high and then bring you down so low. It's strange how people can sit in judgment of others in their relationships when we all stay for our own personal reasons whether they are sane or not. My life is filled with drama, admittedly caused by some of my own personal choices, and that's why I have been working on keeping things together and taking responsibility for my decisions. Traveling this road is exhausting all of my options, although this is what usually gives me the courage I need to move forward and let go, and at some point I have to recognize that I have given it my all before throwing my hands up and declaring victory to *cocaine*.

Going into this relationship with an open mind and wide eyes was first and foremost on my list; I expected challenges but obstacles such as family members, in-laws not wanting to see their brother, my husband, happy, prospering, thriving as a good man in all his endeavors is beyond my imagination. The road I have chosen to take with my man, for my man, has come at great cost, but it's been a lesson well taught by the people who will laugh in his face later, once he's lost me.

I had been friends with Liza for four years when I met Able, she would barf at the things I have compromised my standards to do for him, mainly because she is the opposite of me, Liza will take the closest road, straight out a bad situation. Maybe I should try that road to see how it feels to just let go by running away, no I am a mother and my maternal instinct would not let me in good conscious or sanity take that road.

My mother is unbiased when she says that I give one hundred and ten percent of myself in dealings with people and even more in relationships. Able has been let down so much until he is unable to recognize a come up or the hand that's being extended to him without any strings attached. He has nothing to repay me financially; I just want to see him healthy again. In his addiction nothing I do is enough, his vision is severely obstructed. When Cain is put to rest, Able's sight will be twenty-twenty. By then he will have allowed the drug riddled streets and his parasitic family to suck the life out of him and all that we could have possibly been.

I forgot to mention that Able's work skills are impeccable and his worth breathes a comfortable income; I personally think that's the driving force behind all the enablers. They call for bills to be paid and when he is sober the first thing he says is I have to ask my wife, when Cain is in control those words change to no one

46

tells me what to do with my money. In our case money has become a sore spot having it as well as not having it; his family's pursuit of money is evil, and even though my bloodline is nothing to write home about, his is the worse I have ever seen.

Lying by omission, is the legacy being recorded in this family and I am sure there are other families like this one, but I am not cursed to know them. The Judas kissing, years ago led me to limit my association to funerals only, which in itself is sad.

The main difference in our family is the infighting has to do with control. I know of two people in my family that are struggling with drug addiction. Those two voluntarily stay away because of their personal guilt and shame. The others are control freaks wanting to run everyone else's life while theirs is falling apart. I don't know which is better knowing where your addicts are and feeding into their madness or not knowing so you are not expected to live in their madness. I know that I love them regardless and want them to do better also. I learned that in some cases limiting my association was best in order to preserve my mind.

In Able's case, he is not ready to see or recognize his need to limit contact with certain people. I am now at the point where I have to acknowledge that limits need to be set with him, and I wonder when will I call it quits? How do I say it's over and mean it? When it's too late, when we have taken each other to the ground? Today is one of those days when it feels like I can't bear to go on in a relationship with lingering doubts. Tomorrow I will want to pray a little harder for continued strength and guidance. A week from now I will crave his touch these are all feelings I've experienced over the past several months and I've worn myself out with these highs and lows. As soon as I gain control over the emotional side to this marriage I will think and act rationally but right now I'm speechless. Stealing comfort is what helps me to cope, and realizing that there are other wives that have dealt with or who are currently living with outside problems threatening the health and stability of their families.

I am aware that problems have arisen in families for centuries. I should create a national anthem for women going through something. How about a lifetime movie starring me and Able, featuring Cain, produced by his family and directed by *crack*. I'm sure my character would be the first one murdered, if not murdered, then clinging on to life so that they could finish sucking the life out of me and slowly let me die an agonizing death. The title of this movie should be *Let's Mess up a Good Thing*, I'm laughing that's good.

Yes, finally I am able to say, stupid me married my best friend and begged and pleaded with him not to engage me if it would wreck our lifelong friendship. Able assured me that nothing could ever come between us. Well, well, well here I am all alone in a new state, writing to keep from crying and praying to keep my sanity. That road that I said I'd never take. I've taken it in an attempt to save my husband and protect my children.

Chapter 9

My life became complicated after we said I do. I inherited a massive, uncontrolled in-law population with as much if not more problems as my Able had. I don't even know where to start, with the sister-in-law from the opposite side of the tracks or the baby momma with medical and emotional issues or perhaps the thieving brother-in-law, the back stabbing grandmother or the family killer. Not to mention the slew of cousins struggling with addictions, I promise you I have never seen anything quite like this in my life, it helped when I stopped counting the addicts after reaching a total of fifteen. What was scarier for me was that there seemed to be no other recourse for addiction but acceptance.

I mean we all have our share of addicts and addictions to various drugs and things but substance abuse runs rampant in this family. It's like, normal for them to be shooting, smoking or snorting dope on a daily, no, hourly basis even with the children being at arms' length. They have houses that you can retreat to anytime of the day or night. It's the strangest most dysfunctional

49

thing I have seen in my lifetime and I hope and pray that there is nothing else like this for me to see. This behavior was going on way before my time as an in-law, so I wondered if there was anything I could do to save my husband. This thing is bigger than me and my heart aches for this family, because they have lost so much, and gaining is not even on their radar. Unless it's for temporary pleasure and often it's at each other's expense.

My Able is capable of fighting his own battles in most cases but with all of this activity I just feel that I should not let him fight these demons alone, in a foolish stupor blanketed in false affections. I'm not an expert by any stretch of the imagination I'm just a wife confused and bewildered at the circumstances I'm faced with. The way this script is written couldn't be any clearer than a darken skyline illuminated with celestial bodies, Cain's death is imminent if no one intervenes on his behalf. Right now that person is me, Able's wife, I am all he has, and he is all I want! There are family members and nonmembers who say let his addiction run its course, someday he'll get tired, but that's not the way to help that's a cop out.

Able is used to people opting in and out of his life that is why I have stayed this long. I didn't want him to think my vow to him was insincere or that there was an option to leave a bad situation, because the vow I recited was in sickness and health. That day I committed my healthy heart to his was the moment I accepted the possibility of future ailments. I vowed to see him through any and all setbacks; his addiction is a temporary sickness one that we will work through together. I pray that it's not affecting both of our health.

Hospital Stay

Yeah I was riding along angry as hell
Thinking to myself all seems well
When I experienced an abnormal sensation
Like my facial muscles starting to swell
My neck region began to throb as my heart
Rapidly raced what in the world could this be?
Not me the strong one succumbing to stress
I think it was the limited rest the realm sleep
That my body reject because of all the chaos
Pandemic drama
Irrational Nonsense
I am confined to a hospital bed
Seeing my life flash before my eyes
Is truly a wakeup call
So what if he, she, it we drop the ball
Life does go forward after all
That's what breathing is about
The living not the dead
Taking positive steps to get ahead
Following a path with a level head
Standing strong not being afraid
Of the possible failures of imperfection
Acting childish for fear of rejection
You see no one really blames a child for their selection
Because they are not bathe in maturity
Yes I am lying here thinking about all
The Madness that has gotten me here
On the seventh floor of a hospital door
I maybe down but never count me out

51

For where my weakness is
I can pinpoint the source
Now is the best time to re plot my course
I am the host of instability
As long as I am guided by
Another's inability
To handle their affairs with dignity
That's right grace and dignity
They both work hand in hand
To help me as an able-bodied Woman stand
So maybe it's not the outside chaos
Rather the internal discord
That I am hosting inside of me
Whatever the case may or may not be
I am turning over a new leaf
On this immature tree
Following the seasons as they
Pass by
Manifesting into glorious scenes
Both old and new
Still reflecting the need for change
Never producing quite the same
Foliage but still a lovely sight
Boy what can I do with all this might?
First I must bow my head in humility
Asking that his spirit reside in me
Helping me to bounce back
Out of this rut
Into my infamous strut
There are people who need me
But not as much as I need them

This hospital stay was short but I
Have no intentions on coming
Back especially lying on my back
Down and out with no one to shout
The memories of my stress and unrest
But a cold white sheet fully covering me
And it's not about to end not just yet!

Book Club Notes

Chapter 10

It is unbearable for me to watch him, knowing how much he is missing out on, what he has lost, and what we no longer have, all in the name of drug addiction. From the time I became a mother, my life changed, learning to sacrifice was all that mattered, putting my children first so that they could flourish was never a second thought, so with love I gladly added Able and his child. That was the blended family I wanted, even with the challenges it came with. At this time in life, I realized that making sacrifices didn't mean I had to put myself last, because we all needed proper care and attention.

I also expected tests of endurance in gaining a baby momma. She was sickly, which spells needy. Lauren was not finished with her feelings for my husband, I learned the more I defined her emotional affliction as a woman scorned, the more he denied her affection. How in the world can he speak on her feelings, especially since she relishes at the moment of his relapse into addiction waiting for his drug disoriented calls. I am a woman, I know when holding out hope is all you have. Not to mention that my stepchild has special needs, which you would never know by the way Lauren carries on talking about her own death as if it was about to happen at any moment. Lauren claims that the doctor said she would be dead within three months, but not before she becomes a double amputee.

The futile efforts she is wasting while waiting on the dissolution of my marriage should be directed towards giving her daughter due time and attention. Here's a perfect example of disrespect, Lauren calls Able's phone and if I answer she immediately hangs up when he answers she wants to know if she is around, referring to me. Able says what do you need, she insists he answer the question, if he answers yes she hangs up the phone on him, if he answers no she continues with her lame attempts to drum up compassion for her loneliness. The immature nature of all her calls is disgusting. I have a baby daddy who never, ever calls with foolishness, if my husband answers the phone he is respectful and courteous all the time.

My depression is hidden but it's there. I know that I can make it without him because I'm strong, but I don't want to. I know Able's child and even his child's mother needs him at times. I read somewhere that the definition of father means not giving up, but getting over ones past so that the future of their child should be his priority. It also requires a commitment to the physical requirements, emotional wellbeing and social involvement with both the child and their mother. Some women would say that's a pile of malarkey and that I should give him an ultimatum. I however believe there is an air of reasonableness to that interpretation of fatherhood but that does not lessen my fears. Because a sick woman still has desires for my husband and her intentions are not pure, so how do I give my man to another woman, *oh God please help me.*

Book Club Notes

Non-Sexual Infidelity

I have acted a Fool far too long
Falling for the crafty acts deceptive plays
Belonging
To my bell ma'
Your baby's mother
She is simply paralyzed
Into believing your lies
Prompting her to believe
In her arms you will reside
She started out
Calling my husband "daddy"
Fantasizing of him riding in her "cattie"
The affection she neglected to give
Because of her imaginary sugar disease
How else could she please
A man with a nature to ease
By offering him a piece of fruit
Feeding him sweets from the pantry
Ha! She better come again
My husband is in for the win
Not the layer of sin
she covers him in
Paper thin
Compared to her thick disproportion skin
Even a blind man can peg her bag
Hiding her stench
Soiled and drenched
Cussing in broken French
Sitting on a bench

59

Rather than a chair
For fear it will give way to lies despair
Foaming at the mouth needing air
To catch her breath it all seems unfair

But I was supposed to be the fool
Losing my cool
Sitting on a stool
Waiting for that fool
The one she betted against
Ha! She better come again

Whether he is with her or me
I will always be the champ
That's my life stamp
Call me what you want
Lady or tramp
It does not change my guiding lamp
At least I try living in a spiritual camp
Atheist ain't where it's at
Try him scat cat
Looking like damn it to hell
Sounding the alarm ringing the bell
Can't even sell
The stories he tell
That compel
You too well
Up in tears every time he flee
Ha! You should have asked me
I am the wife!

The one you beefing with
Holding strife
Over my husband
And your used to be
Girl if that's the best you can
Give it up find your own plan
He will never be yours
As long as he wants me
This is obvious,
Ask his family tree.

Book Club Notes

Chapter 11

Help me shut this door that keeps swinging back open. Help me extinguish this fire burning in my heart, how can we go back to being friends after all the hurt and pain, we can't. I cannot imagine our lives, my life ever being the same, and know I'll never love this way again, it hurts far greater than it heals, to love someone so intensely that you began to lack emotional, and physical control over your thoughts. Loves devastating effects lead people to write books, tell stories and marry again for the love of money. When you see me, you see my outer beauty, after you talk with me my inner beauty shines forth and there are no flies on me, yes I can confidently pat myself on the back especially since Able hasn't in a long time.

Any man would have jumped at the chance to marry me, as a matter of fact, I had other more promising suitors, but I was hooked on those empty dreams and broken promises from years ago. I choose Able because I thought he would be like a lion but he's proving not to be one of those courageous, fearless, warriors known for protecting their fold. I know Able is afraid of losing me, on our wedding day he told anyone who would listen how this was the happiest day of his forty years on earth and I truly believed he felt that way; however, time has taken its toll on him actually on us, and even I no longer feel the way I felt on that day. On that day Able was to become my protector, provider, friend and lover for the rest of our lives. That night before we immersed our bodies in marital union we prayed for substance, guidance and peace, we asked God for his forgiveness of all our sins and his blessings for all our future endeavors as we nervously said, Amen. I felt loved, cherished, desired all without conditions.

That night I laid my Able down and made love to his beautiful mind. I engaged him in a pleasure he had never known or knew existed. His body trembled and his heart raced as I followed those big brown eyes of his up and down. He lamented the words I love you over and over again, it meant the world to me that he was being satisfied with every touch of my lips across his chest and around his neck with no control of his reflexes. He asked, begged me, not to stop, as the warm oils traveled down his spine he made short wisps that just intensified my desire to romance him until his toes quivered and quivered they did. It was literally breathtaking for him as he cradled himself in a fetal position the rest of the night and I watched him as he wrapped my arms around his frame. I knew I had taken him there and that was alright with me that's where my motto comes in, *greater later*. I would teach him how to satisfy me, walking him through my mind as he made love to my body and directed the beats of his heart with sensual whispers that would send chills through me.

Now this world wind of chaos has cast a dark shadow over my fairytale future. I am starting to believe the lies, trusting my heart less and less. Neglecting my gut instinct that my grandfather, rest his soul, encouraged me to follow. He preached that to us girls from sunrise to sunset, calling it the alpha and omega.

Writing letters, sending encouraging text messages has become my voice to Able. Putting it on paper affords him opportunity to read and reread my thoughts, feelings and concerns. Maybe in his darkest moments, the words I love you will pop on the light that continues to lose its ability to guide his footsteps. I just want to smile and laugh again, I want my shoulders to feel light again, and want my husband back, the man I married.

Book Club Notes

What Have You Done?

What have you done to your mind?
With the drugs you find.
How did you justify your betrayal to him?
the beautiful frame that once housed your loyalties.
the handsome man that smiled at his own reflection.

What are you thinking?
Drinking out of the devil's cup.
playing with the fire, that leads to burns
so severe that even cosmetics cannot fix.
legions of wicked forces has taken over your once blessed mind
only to find empty chambers this drug left behind.
his glow is gone now he must move on to
the home he has built alone.

He lets no one in but his polluted thoughts
this is the cause of his untimely demise.
it's 8:37 he is missing from home,
you hurt the one who trusted you so
then get angry when she decides to let you go.

Down that valley of death that you are trodden
is a man prodding in shame and blame
for something that no one can change in his lifetime.
stop hurting yourself others too
you know better than to do what you do.
figure out before it's too late
as your life stories the preacher relates,
over your body laid out in class

for onlookers to see, your dead ass.
You had the chance to make it right
to follow your heart and put up a fight
instead you chose to bid a good night
when you close your eyes hitting the pipe
your heart skipped its last beat
that wasn't right
for you to leave me here in this life
as a woman of sadness no longer your wife.

A widow true to her vow

MY HUSBAND DIED YESTERDAY
no one cared
they call ME to handle his final affair
the same people that claimed to love him so
only want to party at deaths door
But
I give them no hope of a festive farewell
he was their problem child my lover and "boo"
to hell with all those onlookers
let them continue to do what they do
this chapter of my life is
over through

Chapter 12

Cain and his thoughts, actions, and omissions can be controlled with proper intervention, but with all that being said, he has to see the need to get help off of his destructive course. It's awful; I being his wife, having to communicate my feelings through drug ravished Cain, begging his pardon to ask Able to free me from this relationship. I want my entitled possessions back, the ones he has suppressed within his addiction: My self-worth, pride, dignity, happiness, joy, hopes, and dreams of a better life. The outsiders see a shining star what they believe to be a devoted wife, establishing her ground, supporting her man, and building their empire one block at a time. Not realizing their assumptions are far from accurate, this blinding darkness of Cain's addiction has taken over my life. I often think what sort of woman have I become to myself in all of this? Until I'm ready to help myself out of this pattern of abuse, I need distance to think things through.

I need my children's laughter and smiles, their innocence is what I have been neglecting to protect due to the outside drama that I've brought into their lives by the choice I made to follow my heart. It's time I let go and focus on restoring a calm environment for me and my children to lay our heads. This story of addiction, co-dependency and recovery is a little strange, a bit chaotic and more irrational than I'm used to, but this is the world people live in, where things are unsure, uncertain and confusing. Only with strong faith will I make it through, therefore, I am determined to keep praying, keep writing and keep my head up. There are no magic wands to erase the words and actions spoken and unspoken in carelessness.

Once you brand a horse it's identified for ownership and that is how this family operates under branding. They want to own something and someone, what they need is a reality check. Able's family intermingles in circles, the ones that produce the negative effects of inbreeding. From what I perceive, there was a lot of swapping going on. I stepped into situations where cousins are actually siblings; uncles are brothers and nephews to each other and grandmothers are aunts if there is any sense to be made of that. Able's confusion is greater than mine, he had to grow up with the stigmatism attached to his family name but I just inherited the pain. It seems to bother me more when people reference me to those people I jump to my own defense as an in-law.

First the sister-in-law from across the tracks, her name is Jezzy short for you guessed it Jezebel, do you know that in the back woods of Mississippi everybody has a nickname. Some of the people living deep in the delta are considered not to be wrapped tight, Jezzy is the definitive example. From the bits and pieces I gathered, Jezzy flirted with insanity in her teens, I didn't know Able's sister existed for about three years because she was remanded to a psychiatric unit for arson when she was around the age fifteen. Able never mentioned her name. This female has an IQ that's equivalent to dumb. She has no idea how a lady should act, she shoots dice, chews snuff, smokes pot and wears dungarees all day every day, if you didn't know better you would think she was a boy.

I personally don't know how she managed to become a mother seeing that laying with women is her personal choice as it relates to her sexuality; I have no problem with peoples choices but why flaunt it in a trashy way. I do however assume that if you are going to do certain things be the best you can at it. Jezzy is the prime example of what a poster child should not be, she's illiterate, trifling and nasty, it wouldn't surprise me if the rumors I've heard about her sleeping with her brother and several of her cousins are true.

This woman had a nice husband, tall, good looking, young and respectful. They were living a fairly comfortable quiet life raising their daughter together. The next thing I knew she quit her job started selling that white girl out of her car, riding around all day with her infant daughter in the back seat. I mentioned greed earlier; her claim was that her husband was not making enough money to support their small family. Lenard had a legal job description making honest money and was proud of his job. You would definitely have to be from the other side of the tracks when you substitute your husband's integrity for slinging dope.

Jezzy's new illegal career meant that she would associate with all kinds of people none of their personalities should have been something that she wanted around her child, but perhaps she didn't care. These shady characters, mostly men were always calling, or paging her for their fix, and Jezzy readily responded. I barely knew her because I had only been in her presence for short periods of time, but there was always something domineering about the way she would speak to others especially the way she handled her husband. It's no wonder the vine said the man worked like a Hebrew slave and when he wasn't working he often went to his mother's house for peace. Relaxing at his momma's table always eased the burdens of trying to provide for his ungrateful wife. Lenard sat for hours playing solitaire, sometimes, bid whiz with his mom if she wasn't busy.

I believe even darkness has a way of letting in a little light; just enough to guide you through or to your end, well here's the light. Several months after she quit her regular nine to five, Lenard, was convinced by a little bird to have her followed. The accusers in the back woods of Mississippi were saying that Jezzy had heavy traffic in and out of their home; I guess the product became popular and her clientele started coming to her, within two days Lenard uncovered his wife's double life as a drug dealing adulterous woman. The things he witnessed firsthand sickened him; the worse being he caught Jezzy in a threesome in their bed as his daughter slept in the living room. This was the ink he needed for a speedy divorce. She had seemingly ruined her marriage over night.

Able and I were almost seven hundred miles away, the lies and garbage she was feeding us about her marriage falling apart had no way to be verified. Lenard was supposedly fighting her and cheating. Honestly it was not on my radar to care whether or not she was being truthful; it had nothing to do with me, so I thought. Later I would find out it had a lot to do with me, because I was now married to the man she clung to in support of her lies and deceit. Jezzy had no problem asking for money, I questioned Able about her finances seeing that she sold dope over her child's head and apparently she was turning tricks. Where was the money?

As a new bride maintaining my household was all I cared about, there were no billboards warning me of the venomous bite of this woman. Able believed every sordid story she told, he had no idea of the mess his sister had caused, some people will read this and think at some point Jezzy's IQ was higher than most, but believe me her ability to rationalize things and place them in their respective places is nowhere to be found. Jezzy acts as if she is developmentally challenged and would be a great candidate for that first of the month check. She is just like her brother when it relates to street savvy, however in the real world of work and intelligence you wouldn't expect her to make it. No one in their right mind would jeopardize the well being of their innocent child by dealing drugs, and allowing these people into her daughters comfort zone, unless they were *certified*. After the light exposed her deviant activities her name was etched in the red clay of Mississippi. She wanted to leave and I along with my husband found her a place nearer to us, wrong, wrong, wrong. She came to the new state with her same old trifling ways, and before long she was stabbing Able in his back. She was hand feeding him dope and robbing me blind, not only did she take from me financially, *I have never in my life experienced someone stealing from me,* devastating me, but emotionally she has stolen my trust, literally dividing my household.

When I tell you she is pure evil there is no other way to describe her. I thought Able and I were doing fine until Jezzy arrived. She said he was already smoking crack, I just didn't know about it. I mentioned to Able what she said and he denied using crack. He confronted her in front of me, and she had the nerve to say she didn't say it like that. I couldn't believe my ears, I guess now I'm the stupid one and the liar. As soon as you think you have things a little stable she adds fuel to the smoldering ashes. That's how she operates, she's sneaky, but she has met her six bit change in me. I am not afraid of her, and as long as I have breath in my body I'll always fight for her brother's happiness. I am not okay with losing the people I love and I know how to fight fire with fire, but in this case she's not even worth the gas it takes.

I can tell by her unconscionable actions that Jezzy knows that Lenard has disappeared from her poisonous reach, leaving her to fend for herself and instead of her asking for another chance she rather do anything and I mean anything to break up another woman's happy home. *Look around I'm sure you will know at least one or more women who have traveled that same road.*

Since Lauren realized that Able had married me, his life long friend, my phone hasn't stopped ringing. Able and I have a love of traveling and when we're gone his phone rings nonstop, his sister is calling with some off the wall nonsense about uncle Duddy, cousin Ray Russell or whoever else, it's obvious that they don't understand the concept of vacation. I have a tendency to take my husband on frequent weekenders; we just get up and go because I can tell when he's tired and frustrated with everybody. His family and baby momma hate our life together. For some reason, they find it impossible to believe that he chose me as his shelter. They think I encourage him to turn off his phone but they forget he's a grown man in all aspects, no one, not even I can tell him to turn off his phone in most cases the phone goes off because he's tired of the foolishness. He turns the phone off because he wants to, the end, bottom line. With all of the calls and drama Jezzy has yet to step back and see the tug of war she is creating, but I guess it's a way for her to escape her own reality. Only after we helped her move did I find out that she was being charged with attempted murder for the poisoning of her husband. Lenard no longer wanted or desired her services. Her life is following a pattern of drug induced insanity. Jezzy seemed to enjoy the status of being recognized as a female hustler, a lifestyle not commonly expected of mothers'. I am justified in my feelings of anger and resentment, wanting to protect myself from Jezzy in not unreasonable. No woman in her right mind would think to poison a man without making sure her plan was fool proof; she has watched the network for women by women entirely too much.

Jezzy's dissatisfaction and misery was being played out by her attempt to break apart my marriage. The game she is playing has been played by many before her, but it won't work as long as I want him. The final outcome for her is a life of isolation; the tangle web she weaves will only trip her up in the end. Able is starting to see her crippling ways and how it has contributed to his continued addiction. As if Jezzy wasn't enough, I also inherited Lauren, the baby momma with parasitic tendencies, she happens to be Jezzy's best friend, of course this wasn't common knowledge to me.

Book Club Notes

Chapter 13

From the time she found out we were married, Lauren has demanded everything from him. Most women would think I'm crazy for allowing Lauren to need my Able, but I rationalized that there were extenuating circumstances involved here. How naive I was and now I am paying dearly for trusting his ability to reason with her and her strong desire to have him one way or the other. Her being diabetic, obese and stressed out all the time had everything to do with the compassion I showed initially. I knew that she was the primary care giver for their daughter who was born prematurely due to the mother's medical problems and his possible addiction at the time. The child's medical and developmental problems were justification enough for Lauren to intrude into my life. I knew she looked at him as her meal ticket for the next eighteen plus years. She whined and complained that Able was a deadbeat dad only to satisfy her own ego. Lauren persists in thrusting her emotional turmoil upon us. She rationalized in her miserable existence the only way to get Able away from me was to concoct sudden illnesses to befall upon their child. Medically it is labeled Munchausen by proxy, the intentional infliction of illness by a caregiver for the purpose of focusing the attention to them, but I called it just plain crazy. With this last incident, I confronted her, questioned her impure motives; she sunk to the lowest stage of mothering, all for the shell of Cain. I don't think she understand what she is doing, she is fighting a married woman over her drug infested husband. The agenda is clear; Lauren never loved Able because she was too busy stroking her ego with Cain's cowardly conducts.

When I would see her I felt nothing but pity, she's not like her friend Jezzy, Lauren is an educated woman who just took a turn for the worst because of her health issues but now she could go to Hell for all I care. She is vindictive and cold with a dependency on my man, wanting to see Cain need and beg her for what I have stopped giving, financially. Lauren is content, satisfied with seeing Able in his addiction, but the fact that I will not hang around for his eventual death is what she clings to. I cannot speak on their years together, but I do know they were together for nine years. Four of, which she clung to Cain while he abused crack, three years he spent incarcerated in state penitentiary and supposedly sober for two years.

Lauren would call if she wasn't feeling well, the furniture needed to be moved, the trash needed to be taken out, the neighbors are making too much noise, you name it, she needed it, rarely did she call for the needs of the baby. For the past ten months I've sat and watched my husband run ragged trying to appease her at my urging, just concerned that no one should have to leave messages of distress, such as the doctor has given me two months to live, I need to talk to you about our daughters future. Oh my goodness how dreadful

78

is that claim. I messed up long time ago when I would tell him to go and tend to Lauren; I don't want her to die because she has a daughter to live for. On most occasions Able chose not to answer her calls, which I figured was not right, because regardless of her complaints she was still a woman with feelings. I was dead wrong for ever empathizing with the other woman. Lately she seems to have some sort of resentment towards me, when I have always encouraged Able to be more involved. Mind you this woman had not met me face to face, but I know that all this anger stems from the lies Jezzy tells, as well as, Able not defending me as he should. If she only knew how Jezzy is setting her up for the ultimate betrayal, Lauren would wise up as I had to do, but she'll find out how untrue their friendship is.

I remember once, how Lauren was supposed to be paying a bill for Able that they had made together, and faithfully he gave her his portion, and unfaithfully she chose to not pay the bill causing Able to this day to have problems with his credit. The least she could have done was give him a warning that she no longer felt obligated to handle his personal affairs. Able fails to see the connection she has to seeing his failure. After repeatedly begging and pleading with him to conduct his own business by means of secured funds he assured himself, but not me that she would never use the funds for any personal reason, well you can guess what didn't happen as he planned, and then I had to hear the bullshit.

I don't understand his mind set; after a few weeks of her calling, sobbing and apologizing, he forgave her, but I the wife always get the backlash for Lauren's needy and deceptive behavior. I think her resentment has a lot to do with her inability to travel, attend school functions with the child, picnic and all the things normal families do. She can do those things with her child if she thought enough to lose weight and manage her health better, but no she'd rather sit around and lose her freedom to move about all in the name of having Able in her grips. All of this has given her the notion that I am stealing her dream of the white picket fence. She felt as if I had taken her man and was trying to replace her in her daughter's life that is foolishness on her part, because I am a mother and I feel like no other woman could steal the love and affection my children have for me, no woman! Lauren has found problems with everything I've done for this child; I made alphabet, reading and writing cards that she threw away when she found out that I was attending parent teacher meetings with my husband. She decided that she no longer wanted him to attend, and school activities became unimportant when she discovered I was taking an active interest in her child's education.

Looking back I cannot see how Lauren conceptualize the, *I took her man theory.* That was not the case. Able and I have been friends for over twenty years and our bond had never been fleeting, eclipsing the belief that I just popped up. The one aspect we did not entertain during our entire friendship was that of intimacy. Able was dead set against sharing me with my husband. I was not going to be another man's wife and Able's girlfriend. Able had to have me all to himself. Lauren was jealous, irritated by me including Able and their child into the lives of me and my children. I did not step into her shoes; I had several pair of my own that fit rather comfortably. I was not replacing her as she foolishly believed. She accused me of stealing the affection of Able and the baby. I would never interfere with a maternal bond. If Lauren continues at this rate of mania her next visit to the psych ward will be involuntary.

I would welcome the new spouse of my ex to help with the growth and rearing of my children if I knew she had their best interest at heart, not this woman, she is truly insecure. There were many days I wanted to tell her to lose weight, get you a man, hire a personal care assistant and get a life. My days however would be cut short if I displayed a flagrant attitude knowing this woman is in need of help.

Now I can see where I should have set limits when it came to her, and around our seventh month of marriage I had reached my limit with them both. We were on a mini vacation and Able decided to turn off the phone, because it was my birthday weekend and he didn't want the phone disturbing him during our activities. He had promised to indulge me all weekend and he did, but I paid for it later. This woman called all weekend and because she couldn't reach Able on his phone she finally got up enough nerve to call my phone, which I did not answer all weekend either, but she left me a message assassinating my character. I now wish I had answered the phone so she could have heard for herself the passion that Able had with his head buried between my legs. The screams that I made when he blew his warm breathe over my thick brown thighs wrapped around his neck, and let her analyze why he refused to pick up the phone, why he enjoyed my nakedness all weekend and didn't give anyone or anything a second thought. Maybe she knows his routine, maybe she misses his warm passion but that's no reason for her to question my integrity as a woman. The message went exactly like this, *I don't know what kind of woman you are, keeping a man away from his child, you are not a god-fearing Christian woman as you proclaim. OH HELL NO!* She crossed that line, calling a man's wife, and disrespectfully presuming that I had something to do with him not being there for his child. Mind you this woman is atheists and has no idea about life and its purpose. I will never forget the nerve of her, she and Able are both going to have to answer one way or another, he for his lack of courage and Lauren for her unbridled tongue. This woman or anyone for that matter should be grown enough to ask the important questions of a step-parent, be civil and respectful of the woman who feeds, clothes and loves your child in your absence. I'm thinking what kind of self-esteem it took for her to leave me that unjustified message, especially seeing that she left none for Able.

I was crazy for allowing her to provoke me, which is exactly the hair raising static she wanted. Getting me amped had become her full time job. She was playing a game that she could never win. Nobody wins at the expense of another, those games are not competitive they are vindictive. I have tolerated considerably too much from these two and more from Able because he is responsible for this mess. My husband is supposed to keep the peace among those in his inner circle; I believe that Able is strong and gifted in more ways than he knows, but he has allowed Cain to limit his power. If Able cannot determine what the support and needs of his wife are verses what help his baby momma needs, then he is not ready to be a husband, because he should know that the wife comes first. In the beginning of our marriage that was how everything rolled, behind me, but how the tides have changed with his addiction overruling all his mental faculties. The Able I know would have never allowed Jezzy or Lauren to interfere. All the hell Lauren had been raising with me had a lot to do with Jezzy's instigation. I have to take some blame for this because a man is only going to do what you allow him to do. He is allowing Lauren to surface continuously by not putting a stop to her unexplained intrusions and daily barging into our lives, which means that I am allowing this madness, too.

I know things had gone too far when I was compelled by territorial rage to question my confidence by confronting them both about what their intentions were for each other? Were they attempting to rekindle a relationship, maintain a friendship, or just screw each other, I wanted to know. Better yet why doesn't she just get over herself and realize that she will only make things worse for her and her child by allowing addicted Cain back into her life. In the process of wanting to destroy my relationship she's enabling his addiction because as long as he's using she can attach herself to his sick mind and control him with puppet strings. She doesn't care. I explained to her the situation and how she should want him to get well if not for their child then just because he's a man, or someone she loves or once loved. She outright told me that crack addiction and Able are partnered for life, with him sitting right there, he said nothing looking tired and irritated. I should have walked away then but, I love my husband.

Book Club Notes

Chapter 14

My girlfriend Liza is a female enforcer. She likes to challenge her testosterone as a homicide detective while embracing her estrogen in displays of motherly affection. I call her *lil gangster*, she enlightened me to the tactics of this woman some of, which my sheltered upbringing shielded me from. Lauren's ass would have been tagged, bagged and laid to rest according to Liza. The first bullshit call she made would have been her last according to Liza, it's just like you *old conservative Liz* with your hands behind your back, you can't win a fight like that. Liza badly wanted to intercede on my behalf, but I didn't think adding her to my sordid drama in a physical way was necessary, besides she was more involved than anyone else, listening to countless hours of chaotic pathetic outcries from her delusional friend.

Neither one of these women cares or even likes Able, for Jezzy and Lauren to tolerate his madness exposes their hatred for Able. Being comfortable with him barely breathing in the ruinous air of addiction is irrational, but what can I expect from those two, and they say they love him. The dense, immature and contemptuous behaviors of Cain, Jezzy and Lauren were wearing down my resistance. I feel tied down, and their assaults on my spirit has grown weary, *Lord just one more request, give me the courage I need to move forward.* Wisdom outweighs ability, *please Lord lift me up out of their midst.* I confronted Lauren and in her ignorance she said that her feelings for my husband are strictly platonic, after all they had a nine year history. All I could do is pity her, because the years they spent together were filled with lies and deceit. Able himself admits to never seeking help or being offered help for his addiction during their time together. Not seeking help was a reflection of their instability as individuals.

I have known Able much longer than Lauren, actually most of my life, and until Cain surfaced I had never experienced Able's darkness. As his wife and soul mate I am obligated to go that extra mile for his sobriety. In all the years that I've dealt with Able I've stood up for him in his recovery, never falling down with him in his addiction, wrong day, different wife. I don't know how she sleeps a night because I am restless thinking about all the awful things that could possibly come from his life's course.

I Know Able and I are worth it, but deep down I'm questioning whether or not it's worth it because he has added all these other people to the problem. We took a vow for better or worse but now we seem to be on two different paths. We are both struggling in our own way. One minute he's suggesting great things and the next he is having dinner with her in a public place; I ask myself why in the hell am I still around. Able is wearing out his welcome in my life quick fast and in a hurry. Lauren has to be fascinated with betrayal

86

because I have heard of the disastrous life they had together when Cain was using, it was no walk in the park, as I am slowly finding out.

When you use people by encouraging and enabling their sickness, in the long term that person will resent you, so I am walking away and I hope that Lauren stops feeding her own insecurities at the demise of Able, if not that dreadful call will come. I guess they expect me to live my life married to the same insanity Lauren lavished in, or maybe they hope that I'll throw Cain back to them. I cannot give them what I never owned. Whether or not he goes back to her to perpetrate the same crime is of no benefit to me. I won't continue in this compromising state of abuse and neglect. *Not I!*

Everything I have done for Able is at no cost to him, so he thinks, but it has come at great cost to me, his addiction is now twenty-four weeks strong. Cain says it's not, but whether or not you're smoking crack for four, sleeping for two, fighting the outside world for five, once you emerge the cycle begins again. He is in a full fledge addiction, his mind is gone. He blames the weather on me, when the car breaks it's my fault, when he's feeling bad it's because I know he's hungry and won't bring him anything to eat and so on. I guess my thieving brother in law stealing an expensive piece of equipment is minute compared to the hardships I am placing on him. Because I won't allow him to use the home that I created for the safety and security of my children as a flop house he thinks that I've abandoned him.

I entered into this relationship with the utmost respect and trust for and of my husband. I think that his family affairs and the negative relationship I have thrust upon me are all due to his desire to establish a close bond. The family

bonds that normally develop during a child's
formative years but I am not interested in
establishing relationships and neither is the
family thief, he does not give a damn one way or
the other about Able, Jezzy or the other siblings.

Snake, as they so fondly call this brother,
lives in an entitlement society of his own where
nobody and nothing matters except for his wife.
This is okay by me since she had the idea to take
him away from his addiction and fortunately for
them they are living well in another state. If
Snake's thieving ways are still evident I know his
wife is content as long as he is not smoking
crack, it's sad when you must settle for the
lesser of two evils.

Chapter 15

Since we've been married I've yet to see Able come out on top when working with Snake. Able is powerful in his trade as a blueprint surveyor, there are not many as skilled. He understands all aspects of a job, but every time he feels overwhelmed or that the job is beyond his control the doubt sets in, and he depends on Snake for advice. Able knows how Snake operates but he still gives him all the credit for being more capable of doing a better job. The script is always reversed when he starts calling in help from his loving brother. He is more than capable of doing an excellent job without reverting back to Snake for his biased opinions. Snake is talented in their trade but every time he enters a business deal with his brother financially Able loses and I'm the one looking at the veins throb in the front of his head, because Snake has slithered his way to the bank vault always cashing a bigger check than anybody else.

Snake is the most unconcerned, unattractive person I know both in an out. His disposition is filthy and he should be the last people on the face of this earth to pass judgment or try to abuse the people that he will eventually need. I ask myself how could Snake steal from his brother, ruin his reputation and curse the ground he walks on while Able still have mad love for him. I could ask Able but he wouldn't know the answer because when he speaks about Snake he claims not to like him at all and then he calls him for help to complete a job. One act of thievery and I'm done. Able is intimately connected to his work, family and crack this seems hopeless maybe I should get the picture and turn my back to this temporary intrusion in my life.

Snake operates under the assumption that everyone around him should be grateful for his presence in their twisted lives. Cocky, self-centered and egotistical he would rather die before he declare Able a better skills men. Able is just the opposite he has a strange sense of empowering others over himself. I guess he is rubbing off on me, because I am vigorously trying to lead him to his power source while draining mine. Here I'm trying to be his staunch supporter, sad commentary of impaired vision. Addictions are strange; oddly enough my addiction to him is being manifested in bouts of confusion and denial. There is no way I can help him when I cannot help myself. I applaud Snake's wife for being successful in at least getting her husband to higher ground away from the deadly influences of his family and the streets that he grew up in. Getting down and dirty is all this clan knows, they have no get up and go, my Able is the exception and that is what they hate. Able's willing spirit is too much for them to handle, they want him sitting on the porch, standing on the corner, or lying in the gutter with them, their whole objective is to slouch, beg, borrow and steal. Hopefully, sooner than later Able will realize his own potential without help, guidance and assistance from outside forces, mainly me.

Maybe he will never be ready to face the harsh reality of addiction, this would force him to cease with the excuses, they will dissipate into thin air, and he will began to breathe truth. Acknowledgement, acceptance, and forgiveness are all part of the recovery process I pray that he understands the attributes of personal will and determination that precede those other qualities. I say get a job and stop living off the systems and others. Cain is stuck in the mire of their lies because he wants their attention; he is searching for something he already has. What he doesn't realize is that sometime love never comes from the source you desire. The love I have for him surpasses any love others have professed to have for him and towards him and it scares him; at least that's how our family counselor describes it. The bloodline love that he is looking for will most likely never come, mainly due to the fact that they have never really been shown true love, they were taught to get it how you live and not how to live decently and love unconditionally. You can't give what you never had.

The thing that has me stuck is the memories we made not so long ago during our courtship. One thing I enjoyed during our courtship was Able's curiosity. I would use words that Able didn't understand so I gave him a dictionary. He was eager to look up the meanings, this was our personal time. He had heard the words but no one had ever used them in the ways I did, at least that's what he would tell me. I knew he would just indulge me with that dictionary sometimes but it was okay with me. The only definition we had to look up constantly was compassion because he would do things and then ask me if he was being compassionate, *oh how I loved those times we spent*

91

together. Till this day he has not grasped the meaning of compassion but I do give him an *E* for effort because trying is better than rejecting the need to learn new things.

Able was eager and open to new ideas moldable, we chose to learn many new things together, it felt good, whatever our hearts desired we indulged in. We would go to the park and wait for the children to get off the swings so that we could swing and then get upset if they took too long. Able and I would drive to the beach on a whim just to walk in the sand barefooted; we picnicked under the stars and fell asleep under the oaks. We did many childish and mischievous things with no questions asked.

I am still trying to figure out what lead to our impasse, why are we struggling to recapture our relationship? How did the life we live together in prayer become encamped by all those undesirable drifters? I recognized their tactics from the onset, they moved from place to place with no real intention of ever building a viable life in one place with that special someone, instead they used the old stick and move, using and abusing their unsuspecting victims, moving on without a trace. Leaving their dirty footprints, heartache, and pain; they are parasites.

Word Confusion

One minute he loves me
The next second he love me not
Or could it be he loves me less
Amid his hypocrisies
In the course of his struggle
In the mist of his battle
There he is saddled
In a word confusion
Or
Should I say?
If you Change the Words you Change the MEANING
Yes, in this case its word confusion
Causing a delusion
Of meaningful understandings
It's all intertwined in
An Addict's Struggle to Let Go
Refusing to
Read
Comprehend
The rightful use of
A Synonym
Is it word confusion?
That you are using
To justify this temporary intrusion
Of your drug abusing
Ways.........
Trying to navigate the word love
Before and during
The relapse in your mind

93

Truly I find
It hard to believe
You once, ever loved me
Because of ....
your sugar-coated
Word Confusion

Chapter 16

Forgot to mention the maternal grandmother-in-law from hell. This woman has never had an ounce of dignity in her bones. For the two decades I have known her she has been a lying, manipulative woman who would not respect the sacredness of anybody's marriage, because she lived with another woman's husband until his death. I will not speak any further on this subject because she is my husband's grandmother but believe you me I could write a book, plus sequels on her unmentionable conduct. Able has strong family ties that are held together by lies, cheating, spouse swapping, drug addiction and more, it's obvious that the problems entrenching this family will always pose major problems for me, when will I get the picture and run for cover?

Then there is his brother Preston, who within a two hour period allegedly murdered five family members in cold blood, would have been six if Able hadn't gotten away. This heinous crime leads me to believe that his addiction to heroin must have been what caused him to commit this act. This was truly the actions of a drowning man. Many have tried to guess what he was thinking. How could he? Why would Preston commit such a horrific act? I sit back and say, did it slip their minds that here we have another family member enslaved to the paralyzing effects of drug addiction. They tell me that his drug of choice normally causes you to slow down but coupled with the mania of X pills on top of the emotional side effects of betrayal, hello do we not get the picture. My brother-in-law had changed over the years, I vaguely remember thinking in my younger teenage years that he favored a famous rap artist, Preston has these defined biceps, plump lips and a beautiful caramel complexion, he had it going on, if that was your type, Preston was well packaged.

From the time I met him, he always wore a smile that told a story but a demeanor that carried a vicious history. Preston was one of those people you would trust in a heartbeat. When he was up, just like my Able he would give you the shirt off his back, but when they were down, Preston and the likes of Cain were the last beast you would want to encounter. This young man, however troubled always showed me much love, never a harsh word or under eye stare, I respected him for that mutual greeting. I was told some years ago that his daddy was a killer down in the delta, if you needed to get rid of a problem Preston's father was the go to man and possibly the reason his mother fell ill. Able expressed hatred toward his brothers' father because he assumed from what he overheard as a child that his violence towards his mother is the reason they were left without a loving hand, her embracing touch and her maternal insight. My husband told me many times the only thing that prevented him from being a killer was age, had he been old enough the deep swampy waters in the Mississippi deltas would have witnessed a modern day execution at his hands. Fortunate for him someone else got tired of his murderous ways and deviant behavior long before Able was big enough to outweigh a gun.

In times pass the old adage made reference to, *the apple not falling too far from the tree*, unfortunately in Preston's case this turned out to be true, but I knew him before his addiction, which I believed fueled the demons I assumed he had just from the story that Able has told me. A few years earlier I seen Preston at his grandmother's funeral and he was looking his same old self, Able was not there and I asked Preston where was he? He said that all week long they had been looking for him but no watering hole produced Able and as usual Preston was the only one that embraced me. He knew how much his paternal grandmother and I shared, we went way back and he understood our connection. Rarely did I ever see him hurt but this day he was agitated. This was to be expected since the woman he had affectionately called momma was gone. He had a deep seeded resentment towards his entire family that I knew nothing about until this unfortunate and unexpected incident.

Of course Preston was captured, but he is pleading innocent, which dumbfounds my husband. Able's anger is ablaze all the time. He is a ball of confusion being the only living eyewitness in the first set of killings. The system that locked him up as a juvenile now wants him to side with them, but that is not about to happen. I try to ease the pain with scripture and as soon as it seems to be working the case takes another bizarre change and I am back where I started. I pray that they resolve these legal issues sometime soon whether or not this case results in a conviction I am not sticking around for the unknown. When the verdict is read somebody is not going to be satisfied, there is going to be a definite backlash and possibly more senseless murders, it's not worth the sacrifice.

The thing with me boils down to my inner person. When I am with Able my heartaches, when I am without him my heartaches and for the past several months of trying to figure this thing out, I don't' know, which is worse, his constant presence or his agonizing absence. In the back of my mind, it's telling me to run as fast as I can, however my feet are planted in helping my husband see his way through the torment and turmoil he is experiencing. If only Able would stand up and give me a positive sign that isn't fogged by his fear of losing his grip on the only person that is determined to hold him accountable not only to others but to himself, me. Jail and death resounds in my mind daily, I see no other options for him and it breaks every fiber in my being not to think that I've done all that I could to help protect and support my man. I pray for peace for his troubled soul, I pray that God delivers him from his crushed spirit and I pray for wisdom to comfort my husband when all I want to do is chain him to a fence until he regains his sense of purpose. Realistically speaking, my Able has lost his self-respect in those streets with the only person that matters himself.

I wonder what a man can gain from numbing his mind temporarily to reality. How can a man justify losing control of his ability to speak? Why would a full grown man follow another man into a dark alley only to emerge a paranoid piece of garbage? Trash, refuse, or garbage, no matter what you call it once you inhale you become worthless; whether it's for a minute or an hour. You have chosen to transform your status as a respectful human being to something lacking honor. Able agrees that in using drugs he renders himself helpless so what's the problem? Able doesn't believe in the promises of inpatient rehabilitation saying that it's a waste of time. What he has failed to realize is that in rehabilitation there are no promises moving pass addiction it requires individual will and determination.

I do trust from what I have learned in attending support groups that Able has to be the one to decide that he is ready to remove the taste of crack cocaine from his mouth; they tell me that it's a losing battle, but I believe otherwise. I have full trust and faith that my prayers will not go unheard, and when Able starts praying again his prayers will not go unanswered. I will never stop my prayers on behalf of my baby; in the unfortunate event that we decide to go our separate ways, I will still pray for his health and well being to be restored. Never would I want to see any less for him, Able is trapped; I ultimately have the interest of my children and my sanity to protect and I find myself doubting his place in this equation.

Book Club Notes

Chapter 17

I've always known how Lauren plays on the emotions of my husband but she sinks lower and lower with each ploy, now she is claiming that his affections for their child is only surface level and his inner father will always be a deadbeat. Why would she question this man's love for his child? Since Able takes everything personal her accusations leave him doubting his own ability to parent from a different household, but that's crazy, because we have always included our children in everything we do. My trying to reassure him of her mind playing tricks fall by the wayside, I have seen him interact with his child and Able is a great father, like many parents his parenting skills may need refining from time to time but overall he does good things for the growth and support of their child.

My job as wifey is difficult most times, I often reflect on the choice I made to bring my friendship with him to the next level, and I really believe that my life would be easier had we not married but what was the alternative, shacking? With no legal commitment to each other

101

and the knowledge that we could leave without strings attached, *I don't think so*. What would my children have thought about their mother settling for less when I've always tried to teach them the value of respecting themselves first? The focus of this woman, me, started with a vision, from the onset of this relationship I pictured a successful, fun-loving family life with goals and plans that would manifest into genuine love and trust among all the family members.

Able would say he still desires to live the rest of his life with me but as it stands right now I'm waiting for him to take charge and make a manly decision. If I had a dollar for all of the times Able has failed to stand up over the past several months I would be well on my way to easy street. I recognize his desire to do better but his motivation is not there or rather he's looking for motivation in the wrong spot. His bloodline is not interested in stimulating each other; I don't think he is ever going to get that through his stubborn skull. Able lay with me at night and pour out his fears. I ask him to recall the times when we talked about having a meaningful life, living a comfortable existence in a peaceful and tranquil setting with our children. It all sounds nice and simple enough to accomplish when coming from a sober and healthy spirit, however the nature of addiction is beastly, causing these emotional upheavals in Able's mind.

There is nothing neat about the disruptions we are experiencing; my world has become tainted by the ugliness of addiction. I'm going to give Able time and space, which I think will enable both of us some breathing room to evaluate and analyze our futures either together or apart. You know how you purchase something and then you have buyer's remorse, well I see this as our grace period. The situation I'm facing with my love has been the most unsettling thing in my life to date, it has superseded hurricane Katrina and they say that was the worst human/natural disaster in this country, but they have not encountered this hell on earth. All day, every day, I wonder can I survive this nightmare that I'm witnessing as it plays out. One minute I'm doing fine and the next I'm an emotional roller coaster, but I see this as my fault, not being able to muster up enough strength to walk away and not look back. It's shocking to look in the mirror and actually have those feelings of regret stare back at me, without a doubt I should have waited on love.

I have an associate, Candice we met immediately following hurricane Katrina in a Fema assistance lines outside of Mississippi. We were complete strangers who within hours shared pieces of our life story with each other. She said I was such an inspiration to her because in spite of me losing a lot, I kept moving; not dwelling on what was lost instead being grateful for the lives of my children and myself. She was experiencing a similar situation at that time and needed a shoulder. I opened my arms and heart to her and now I have a better understanding of what she was going through with her son, his nightmare is now my husbands' problem. The stories she would tell were truly unbelievable. My jaw dropped every time she confessed how her living was equivalent to hell on earth.

I now grasp her emotional state in a new light and can empathize with her pain. There are days when I find myself having difficulty catching my breathe, gasping for air that seemed plentiful just moments earlier, pulling to the side of the road blinded by the water pouring from my eyes, shaking uncontrollably at the thought of never getting my soul mate back. It's scary. Able has no feeling left after Cain has ingested that poison, and I'm left thinking; how he could feel anything, while under the influence of this drug? In my struggle to rationalize an irrational situation, I called upon God, and next I called Candice really as my last resort because no strong woman wants to involve others in her fight, call it shame or pride but at this juncture I'm neither, I'm desperate. I have been clinging to my own thoughts, trying to make sense of it all and now that this thing is barreling down on my physical health I know I cannot fix it.

Candice returned my call, because she knew immediately that there was something happening in my life, she said, *talk to me, I've seen your pain for weeks now, I know that look of insecurity, you can confide in me I'm here.* All I remember was sobbing like a wounded animal trapped and scared. She listened never saying a word. She allowed me to do what I had needed to do for weeks, let go. Before I could tell my entire story, she encouraged me to always display a strength when dealing with Cain, she said people in addiction thrive off your concern for them and Cain will play mind games for as long as he knows I'm saddened by his behavior and he'll continue to act and behave in a way contrary to his best interest. What she said was nothing new, my mom and aunts said the same thing in the way of never letting a man see you cry. Candice pointed out how my husband's thoughts and judgment was obscured and this impaired his language and whatever he said I was not to take personal.

Was my appearance that dreadful, I had not begun to tell my story, was she psychic, had she heard something on the streets, what, had Cain's disease aged me to that extent. I had no idea my body language was compromised, I guess wearing it well had worn me down. During the time after Katrina, I had shared my fears with her concerning a possible chance of relapse, which was the only thing that frightened me about marrying Able in the first place, but how could she know my worst fear had come true. I certainly didn't think this would happen and if it did, not this soon into our young marriage. I asked Candice, how did she survive the grueling absence of her sons ability to think and act rationally, how did she make it through the days and nights when she had no idea where he was, if he was safe, hungry, cold, scared? I wanted to know if she used the tough love method and if she did how long did it take to work.

I asked so many questions that I know Candice felt overwhelmed by my greenness. Candice said she tried everything but the tough love tactic was the hardest decision to stand by. As big and mighty as my Able seemed, when Cain was roaring my deepest fear was that someone would hurt him while he was vulnerable and the injuries could be fatal. The questions I asked seemed stupid to me but Candice encouraged me to ask what I wanted to know, I needed to know. It didn't matter to her that I was not street savvy; she said most people are not knowledgeable when it comes to the dark activities of drug addiction. I wanted to know if it was normal for me to wake up in a panic, heart racing, and skipping beats, because my thoughts had me seeing Able hurt and calling for me to help him. I shared with Candice how I felt as if a gunshot was piercing my heart, and as I clenched my hand against the wound trying to stop the blood from pouring out of my body, I realized it had been years since I've worried this much about anyone dying. I wake up wanting to cry but after the initial shock wears off, I realize that it was only a dream.

My father was mentally ill after his discharge from the military and I worried

constantly about his safety. Able reminds me a lot
of him. I had many sleepless nights worried that
someone would hurt my father and they did. It is
hard to say but I was at peace when I buried him.
He was a tormented soul and his death released me
from the pain I was experiencing watching him
behave like a mad man. The same holds true with
Able his soul is under attack by an addiction he
claims to derive no pleasure from using.

Chapter 18

Candice acknowledges that she experienced similar feelings; the feeling of disbelief as though you're watching your life pass in front of you. This must be what people describe as an outer body experience. I told Candice how I also see myself in all black at someone's funeral and I'm frantically jumping to see whose lying in the coffin, the only person missing is my best friend, the parlor is packed with relatives and friends but I'm confused, because I can't seem to find my baby, where is he? Who's in that coffin? Why am I on the front row? She listens to my pain and sighs as if she definitely knows the feeling. For hours I recount my horror stories and for hours she listens as I express my fears, my hopelessness and despair, she assures me that there are many women who have and are currently experiencing this nightmarish ordeal.

I continue with my uncontrolled ramblings about how I feel unloved, unwanted and betrayed by Able's choice to use crack cocaine rather than be with me and our children in a healthy and safe capacity. Cain's words are cold and meaningless,

107

leaving no room for an optimistic future. I ask
him if I'm holding out hope for nothing, is there
a light at the end of this tunnel. She assures me
with her compassion and promises me that my faith
will carry me through no matter what the outcome.
I'm reassured by Candice's commentary and relieved
that I'm not crazy, unloved or unwanted; it's the
drug that's talking and saying all those awful
things. I ask Candice why I feel cut every time he
offers no direct answers; again she tells me it's
the drug and his craving for it.

Candice says that his denial only proves
that his addiction is alive and active, in full
swing. She expresses a genuine concern for my
inability to recognize the complexity of substance
abuse. There are various facets to addiction and
factors that contribute to the ongoing struggle. I
was not aware of who I was fighting, it's not just
the narcotic it's Cain, his family, and Lauren.
Because Lauren has his baby she basks in his fall
enabling her to throw salt in his infected wound.
She really enjoys seeing this black hole in Cain,
because his addiction gives her the green light,
providing her proof that no one will have him
except her. In Lauren's sordid mind, his using is
gratifying, because she can control him, and
allowing him to smoke crack guarantees that he
will remain in her life.

Jezzy is running her mouth nonstop talking
about how stupid he is and that he should go home
to his wife and Able, poor Able is lost. She is as
surprised as I was in noticing how his family
operates and she honestly told me that she has no
idea as to how I should respond to those outside
factors that claim to have so much love for Able
but are willing to sit back and watch him commit
suicide. Those waters she did not have to tread,
unlike marital vows, which can be terminated at

any time, Candice's maternal instinct would never let her give up or let go.

Candice suggested that I have a conversation with Lauren, woman to woman; I quickly shut down that idea because there would only be one woman big enough to entertain a positive intervention. Of course I had tried that! On behalf of my step child I would have to do and say the right thing, because no one else has Able's best interest at heart.

Candice has continued to listen and help me with every passing day; there is no rest for my weary soul. A new situation arises everyday and I'm faced with what seems like endless sucker punches, if it's not Cain, its Lauren, if it's not them it's Jezzy. Getting over hurdles and facing obstacles has become my career. I had to stop to think about what Candice said; *Addiction is a monster uncontainable with love alone*. I thought love conquers all! In light of this world's complexities I guess it's only God's love that can conquer all, when I meditate on those words I see the correlation between fantasy and reality. I asked Candice when that statement became real for her. She said when she stopped trying to rescue her son and found options to help him save himself. She called it her aha moment and suggested we attend a meeting together that night.

Book Club Notes

Chapter 19

Candice and I met later that week at a hotel, which had several ballrooms. I was thinking there could not possibly be a need for this many rooms to discuss drug addiction. To my surprise this was an annual convention of Narcotics Anonymous and each room had a different subject being discussed. I wanted to sit in all of them, but Candice had signed us up for a particular seminar; the door greeter said, *welcome to Lovers in Limbo*. The room was filled to capacity with people from every background imaginable; I was shocked that there were this many people. There must have been close to a hundred round tables, and they put us in groups of ten. The speaker said this portion of the seminar was always well attended and today no one would leave without the tools needed to save themselves from the impending crash of their love ones demons. I thought this is where I wanted to be. I want to survive the crash, but the only way for me to do that was to get out of the vehicle. That is exactly what the small groups discussed. There were nine lovers in limbo at each table with one addict, and their advice was to decline the ride even if it meant a long tedious walk up steep hills, roughed terrain, and scorching temperatures or freezing rain.

Every thirty minutes the lone addict moved to another table joining a different group, and each addict had the same message just from a personal perspective. Those four hours ended with me in a renewed spirit. I was enlightened by their personal journeys and how their recovery began with remorse and regret for the pain they had caused to both themselves and the people that loved them. Some of the recovering addicts made it through their ordeals with a bitter sweetness. Being able to live sober is the best recovery; however, some have had to do it alone, because they lost their families. The amazing thing about that is none of them were angry towards those who chose to walk away. This was an awesome experience; one that I will carry with me forever.

I have to say, thank you Candice, there were many days and nights that I would think homicidal thoughts, wanting to inflict some sort of pain, but that's not who I am or who I want to become. To hurt the man I love or his baby's momma would not solve anything. In due time, I know just as well as they know their reaping is emanate. Candice you were, no you are, a life preserver and one of my most treasured friends. When I was drowning, you offered me a way out, even though, I had faith my test was burdensome but you led me back to God's unchanging hand. Your genuineness, and the fact that you never sugar coated what needed to be said, and was willing to share with me your similar experiences have me forever grateful to you.

How can a woman measure her breaking point? When it's too late, or when there's no room left for apologies? When his lies fall to dead silence?

112

I have concluded there is no certain time, place, or occurrence, but I will know by the answers I give when Able no longer occupies my thoughts and my heart. This will be my aha moment. Then I will know.

Book Club Notes

Chapter 20

Today I woke up at five fifteen, which is becoming a regular pattern for me, and I thanked God for allowing me to open my eyes in more ways than one. I slept rather peacefully even through the multiple phone calls and outrageous voice messages. Cain's erratic behavior finally unleashed a world wind of accusations that I never thought I would hear coming from his mouth which loosened his grip on me. Speaking under the, influence as he so commonly does these days has lead him to the wrong woman at the right time. In Cain's cowardly fashion, he let me know just how he feels about us. He said Lauren was the only person helping him pay his bills, and that as his wife I should have paid them. Even though he was smoking up the little income he had. He said she was helping him see his way clear; I expressed my frustrations in a calm manner by thanking him for giving me a chance to heal this open wound that he has been pouring salt in for too long.

This probably shocked the devil out of him and for two days I didn't hear from his stupid ass. He must have been contemplating how he was

going to get his foot out of his mouth. I vowed
never to dial his number again, and almost
instantly the headache that was lingering seemed
to subside; this was a welcomed change. The pain
had been a constant annoyance and I couldn't put
my feet on the floor in the morning without
feeling lightheaded. I'll never forget the level
he sunk to; speaking under duress as if he had no
common sense at all or no other alternative than
to call me his wife with bullshit. I know no other
way to let him go but to stop allowing him my
precious time, so I accept his decision to stay
with her and their child although he is still
adamantly denying having any affection towards
her, *liar*.

This day I have given to him, but tomorrow I
will began to live for me again. I have mixed
emotions as I look at our wedding album while
remembering the day when he told the world how I
had given him the second chance of a lifetime and
claiming this was the best day of his life except
for the birth of his child. Honestly, I had never
seem Able smile as brightly as he did watching me
walk down what I now know to be the longest walk I
would ever take. He gazed at me all night with his
sparkling brown eyes. I knew he wanted to feel my
body against his, and we were both ready to
connect as husband and wife. He whispered all
night in my ear; how much he loved me and
appreciated me for loving him more.

Sadly, the once strong, viable, intelligent,
and attractive man has lost his shine; you can
hear it in the ramblings of his voice, and see it
in the bleeding of his eyes. The shell of a man he
has become. I know the day is not far off when my
pain will be gone, when my smile no longer covers
the anxiety I feel; I have read that moving and
staying busy will help push the walls that have
been closing in on me go back to their foundation.

116

Refocusing my time and energy on the internal repair of my spirit will only be successful if I stick by my vow of not dialing his number, but I question making that vow when the original vow I made to him holds more weight. The commitment we made as young adults was to remain friends no matter what, but that was before the oath we took and the vow we made under God. I had chosen to stick by him in sickness and in health. I remember from when I was a child that it was better to vow not than to vow and not live up to your promise. It is hard being in this place and time where everything seems wasted.

Not answering his calls has always been hard for me; the first instincts I have are wanting to hear his voice and knowing that he is alive, even though, his tone with me lately carries a disheartening rage. Do I need to pray more? I know that strength and faith abounds in those who keep asking for it, and I need it more than ever. Learning to love me fully without the security of a man is something essential for my mental recovery. You hear people talk about skeletons, but I've always felt as if no skeleton could come back to haunt me, but Cain is my skeleton. I feel haunted by his presence; the things I have done all in the name of love for him and with him, and now he chooses to have selective amnesia.

His addiction has caused him to hide behind the times I stood by his side as a partner, stood behind as a support, and stood in front of him as a protector. Able is not the man I once knew and I can only say so many times how it hurts so bad that I can't eat without bingeing, or speak without crying; why have I allowed this addiction to transform my present? I have to do some soul searching. In time, I believe the season will change, and with it my feelings and insight will guide me to normalcy.

It's been two days with no Cain or Able, but here I go again, I'm strung out, and must have lost my mind. I have gone too far in my acceptance of his lifestyle. I feel extremely saddened by my inability to *Let Him Go*! I don't need him, I want him, I've always wanted him from day one, but Cain never allowed me the time and space, maybe that was my clue, but some twenty one years later here I stand. My wanting him has cast a shadow over my entire being. He refuses to comprehend the magnitude in which his sickness has left me without sufficient energy to thrive most days. Cain weakens my soul, zapping all my strength with his foolishness. I pray from sunrise to sunset that God removes me from this situation even if I don't know how to remove myself. This is the diary of a mad woman looking for a way out.

FROM

I write from my pain and never my joy
In his house the darkness he employs
Swallows my glow and hinders my steps
Leaving me unsettled with no time for rest
Whenever I am near him I am weak
Broken and feeble like a motherless child
I think I am in bed with a mild concussion
this time from all the fussing
over foolish nonsense and stupid discussion
over others importance in his mind
seizing the precious time
he should be giving toward
aging his finest of wine
instead he cast me to the side
in an old recycled barrel
where I am kicked around by
visiting tourist
until one day
connoisseur of world renown
taste eyed this lone barrel on the floor
near an open French door
where just a hint of light
shone on the bottom right
of my sealed lid
you see he being a gentlemen
from neighboring Carrolton
had seen the seal of worth
before at a winery near berth
just off Cape Cod

119

ah ha you thought I was paused
well to say the least he picked me up
brought me home and housed me
in his personal vault
where he eyed me every day
touching me
testing for the proper
temperature
pressure
weight
making sure that I would be
more than smooth to taste
refreshing to inhale
you see one man's trash
is
another man's treasure
it's all in how you handle your liquor
beauty is only skin deep and sex is what you make it
if your mate love you because you are good to them
and good for them the sexual possibilities are endless
there are no limits except for the ones you place
because of lies and deceit
treat it with truth and see what it will not do
A woman's love in spite of pain
A man's greater gain

Chapter 21

Heartbroken by every move Cain has made in this lethal addiction, I have been forced to bear up under conflicting emotions, to surmount, to be combative, causing a strain on our marriage and weakening my womanly testament. The only definition I knew for heartbreak was listed in *Merriam Webster*. I sat alone for days trying to define my feelings, only to surface with nothing remotely resembling human intelligence. Then in a burst of animal like rage I began to define myself in the distresses of both my mind and body. What I composed during my lapse in sanity would be my greatest breakthrough to date.

Heartbreak, heartbroken, heartache is the ultimate feeling of betrayal by someone you intimately loved and trusted unconditionally. The heartache stems from the core of our being raped repeatedly by our confidence in other peoples contaminated beliefs. It is the unhappiness of our hearts, the muscles that tighten under stress, the migraines that mitigate a visit to the emergency room in the middle of the night, the minutes when the second hand on the wall seem stuck, the

telling tale of raccoon circles underneath those
tired and restless eyes, the tears that come from
nowhere while riding the public transit, the
numbness that proceed the rapid shakes, the knees
that are sore from kneeling all night in prayer,
afraid of the future, sinking in the past,
drowning as you speak. I need not say anymore!

What's even sadder is that I know scripture
and I know God is carrying me. I know he is fond
of me, but as long as I praise him in the morning
and curse Cain at midday I will never receive my
full blessings and answers. I ask that his word
guide me to greener pastures, and I beg him to
forgive me for not always saying and doing things
accordingly. I ask all these things, and then at
night I hunger for this man's touch, how sad of me
to desire him for more than two decades then
loathe his existence today.

I have become an enemy to myself not being
content enough in my own person to relinquish the
title of nurturer, protector, and lover of a man
who is afraid to face life in sobriety. There
again I've said it; I truly fear not having that
bond of physical intimacy with the only person
I've ever desired as passionately as I desire
Able. The way I feel when he is lying in my bosom
is unique in that I can never get enough of his
boyish inexperience, unadulterated agility,
whispering words, or gentle thrust says nothing to
his bearish statue. The soft caress of his mighty
hand along the tip of my breast, send chills
through my already weakened frame. His lips
covering the opening of my excellencies and his
warm breathe passing over my vulva is enough to
set off an instant orgasm without his tongue
penetrating a depth uncalculated by his own
imagination. It exudes a sound out of my inner
parts that I've only heard when Able has caused my
body to perform that climax that you only get in

122

your maturity; lying in my bosom is where I want this man. That's why I can't' seem to let go. I'll miss his persistent groping when he's trying to find every pleasure point imaginable to me. His refusal to stop until I am well pass my satisfaction is literally breathe taking, I think I'll create a new word, *Sexified*! Our chemistry is magical when we make love there is nothing our minds can foresee to stymie the passion, the one common ground that we've grown to share. I cannot tell you what he sees in my eyes but in his eyes I witness his stimulation; the way his pupils dilate when it's almost there and when I interrupt his completion, the way his eyes constrict, and his heart pounds once I allow him to climax. The tremors in his legs, the arch in his back and the releasing of his seed seeps inside of me for a few more welcoming moments, and finally his appreciative sign of satisfaction. No woman could ever take that/our/my connection. There are no lights off or eyes closed when I love my man and he loves me back.

In better times my girlfriends would always ask me for advice, and I've always said it's not what you do lying down, it's how you make it standing up, but for the first time in my life I'm having to try to make it standing up, absent the lying down portion of my marriage. There is a quiet storm brewing in the heart of a woman that desires companionship. From my mid teen years I had this yearning, but I didn't understand it, for me that was confusing enough, then I met Able and that quiet storm emerged as a passionate mission. I wanted him. I had him; the chemistry between us was magical, but what I later figured out was that young love was nothing more than lustful carrying on without full knowledge of the implications associated with unprotected sex. We had sex whenever and wherever from the first day we met he would want it and I would give it. Never once did

I give consideration to the meaning of lying down with another human being, or where this would lead me. As I grew, the meanings as well as feelings associated with this experience changed, and I realized that our behavior was immature, because we were both acting like irrational children; wanting what we wanted when we wanted it. It's sobering when one can grow up and see when, where, and how you made mistakes.

Chapter 22

The calls usually start when Able is feeling an air of guilt; knowing that if he does not call me in the course of a day I may be getting stronger. He knows exactly what he's doing, throwing me a life line, so that I don't move too far ahead. His lies and deceit are getting the best of him, but as long as he has a cool place to rest his head his mind will stay altered. His excuses are old and my ears are numb to the cold stiff breezes of his fairytale schemes. How long will I sit, stand, and lay down in this mental state? I am clueless as to his deliverance, or whether he has one waiting for him. I ask Able if he recalls better days, and the tears he fights back tell a story. He's afraid to tell his story. In this moment, time, and space I'm oblivious to my calling in his life.

I'm certain that this relationship is not just for a season because of the history we have together, or maybe it was for a season, and I wanted more. God's plan for me may be different than my plan for myself. I try to accept the truth that is staring me in the face; both men and women make choices that suit them, and no matter what a person says or does individually we all make our final decisions based on our personal thoughts. I can only change myself and Able has to want to change himself, but until then my endeavors are striving at the wind. It's hard not to worry and frustrating to watch either directly or indirectly. The knowing or suspecting has engulfed me like the suddenness of a wave that appears easy to handle, but clashes with such great force that it takes your breath away sweeping your feet from underneath you; it's an awesome sight to see unless you are the one being carried away.

In my moments of weakness, I want to pick up the phone and dial his number, because I miss him so. My heart and my hands tremble at the thought of leaving him a message detailing the outcry for relief of my broken heart, but I know this will only fuel his power and weaken my battered mind. I want to tell him how he has opened up wounds that had healed years ago. It took a long time for me to get over the idea that we were not going to be. In actuality, I have nothing to tell him about my stupidity! The *shoulda', woulda', coulda'* argument is voided in this instance, because I knew my Able still had problems. They may not have been drugs, but his family matters and abandonment issues are worst now that I have pacified his hurt and justified his behavior, so what defense do I have left? None!

The questions I need to ask myself are: why have I allowed Able to consume my life with drama, what can I do to get my righteous mind back, how can I walk away, how can I stay, and not resent him for disappointing me, or abandoning me, lying to me? This shell of a man that I've cared for no longer desires the life that God has given him. His depression, ignited by the sudden and unexpected flashbacks from witnessing several

126

murders and being a survivor has his mind twisted and my life in shambles. Able is aware of God's powerful hand so I'm puzzled by his ability to give in to Satan's world. The lies, deception, and pain are overwhelming to me, how Able keeps up this façade only he knows.

From time to time I see his future in my daydreams and nightmares. It's scary knowing the goodness and greatness that lay dormant when Cain is running rampant. Watching the body absent the mind should be a wake-up call for me even if he isn't ready to change. We are living apart in the same house, weird but true. I am here and Cain is there, wherever, that is for him. Slowly I am allowing his destructive behavior to lead my mind astray; how crazy is that? Perhaps my reliance on my God needs a tune-up, because I know he is able, I know his love, I treasure my relationship with him, all because he has carried me through some dark and lonely nights when the devil was riding my back. He will never forsake me as this man of flesh has. Could it be any clearer? I need to wait on my God and allow his word to pacify me when I am hungering for my Able's attention and wanting his hand in prayer. When we prayed together, I always knew everything would be alright and now I must pray alone, but I know it will get better. Able knows that I would do anything in my power to help him stand.

I want to tell him how broken my spirit is, how the river of water I've cried has crest into a flood of instability, how I am on the verge of asking for a house call, because I can't leave my bed, how I need to regain my sanity but what good will it do, when he has lost his way. All of the, I love you, miss you, and need you have fallen on the ears of addiction.

I hurt when he doesn't answer my calls, it's been eleven days, thirty-five minutes and forty two seconds since I've heard from Able and I'm frightened for him, but I'm gaining some strength. My girlfriend warned me against finalizing the relationship but I need closure. She's speaking from what I have willingly chose to disclose, so it's hard not to want an end to this pain when I know the true depth of what I am experiencing. She asked me to remember better times and the love we shared.

I know how this man, my man usually handles emotionally charged words such as love. It's only since his recent relapse that he has spoken that word loosely and without thought. Able has always been a quiet man, a great listener, before mumbling a word he would sit back and think, perhaps even getting at you later with his thoughts on a matter; what I often call over analyzing the situation. He is reluctant to recognize and yield to things that are beneficial; this has caused him more pain than I guess it could ever cause me. I hope and pray that in the near-near future Able regains his composure, finds his way, and turns the spotlight towards his endless possibilities. Able being a strong willed individual is posing a problem for him at this point in our lives. Where is that strong man of mine? I wonder.

My girlfriend called today and asked if everything was alright, I said out of frustration, if everything was all wrong ain't nothing I could do about it now, we both laughed. I'm amazed at the fact I can still laugh, because I feel so bad, but it helps me to remember what people have said to me for years and, that you are a survivor Liz. I know I'm special, because people have always remarked about how I light up a room and my take charge, make it happen attitude precedes me, if

128

only they could see me now. Wrapped up in sorrow, stricken with pain and devastated by what I thought was my true love.

During our phone conversation my girlfriend mentioned how she is learning to use her negative energy around the house cleaning, redecorating and gardening, otherwise she would hurt somebody. I laughed again as I followed with my own version of *get the gun* and how for the past few months my thoughts gravitate from normal to insane in less than sixty seconds. Honestly it feels good to let out a few chuckles. I want to ease out of this situation with my self-respect, but it's unlikely because I am enraged most days, and my Christianity has left the marrow of my bones, fueling the fire burning within has caused me to say and do things that have been out of my character, and if I ever want forgiveness for the can of whip ass that I am about to open now is the time to recite the twenty-third Psalm.

The LORD is my shepherd; I shall not want. 2 He maketh me to lie down in green pastures: he leadeth me beside the still waters. 3 He restoreth my soul: he leadeth me in the paths of righteousness for his name's sake. 4 Yea, though I walk through the valley of the shadow of death, I will fear no evil: for thou art with me; thy rod and thy staff they comfort me. 5 Thou preparest a table before me in the presence of mine enemies: thou anointest my head with oil; my cup runneth over. 6 Surely goodness and mercy shall follow me all the days of my life: and I will dwell in the house of the LORD for ever.

Able called this morning sounding sad and pitiful; I asked myself how long is he going to ache? How long am I going to ache with him? We are still one, and his pain is my pain. When will I let go of his pain to fully nurse mine? Hopefully real soon, because I am tired of these calls and my ability to turn away when he calls is not there. I know I'm going to have many moments where I feel abandoned, because Candice mentioned some time ago that I'm grieving what was.

Candice's son is doing better but it's a constant every day struggle to forgive himself for all the harm he caused to others and himself. You see he's living with AIDS now and it's no walk in the park. I keep my Able in my prayers, and hope he comes to his senses before his life is changed forever. Honestly I don't know how Candice made it through all the horrific stories and situations she found herself dealing with. That's why I cling to her insight and cherish her heartfelt responses to my anguish. She mentioned to me something about support groups that both men and women attend to talk about their frustrations dealing with love ones and their addictions. She suggested I attend a few groups with her. Candice says I'll feel better knowing that my Able is not the only one struggling, battling addiction, and that I'm not the only one in love with a person who seems not to love themselves.

I'm frightened for him all the time knowing the problems that almost always follow addiction and recovery. It's not just the physical damage, but emotional trauma that can sometime drive a person to live a life guilt ridden. Able once told me he never knew a love like this. I've never known a love like this either, bombarded with almost criminal attacks; hell I guess in some ways they have been criminal.

I recall several months ago the air outside was brisk; I think it was mid-winter when Cain returned from a binge with no money and no vehicle. He had been gone for days seemingly trying to suffocate himself with every inhale of the pipe. I was floored at the nerve of this man, and wondered had he lost his mind? The only reason I said nothing was because of those support groups I had been attending where they encouraged me to say nothing, so I just turned and walked away. I left him at his spot where he slept for four days then he called for a ride to his vehicle and I obliged. You see by this time I was moving forward, so I thought. Cain went to retrieve his property and an altercation ensued; I was caught up in the middle of a gunfight on the upper eastside. I could not believe what my eyes were seeing and although I could hear Cain telling me to pull off; I couldn't move. Frozen in time is what I can call it today but then it must have been sheer fear. It was like looking at the filming of a movie transpiring in slow motion but at the speed of light. Whatever the disagreement was, I thought for sure somebody would need an ambulance. I was finished! Able had to move on and I meant every unspoken word.

For the next week we had no words for each other, my heart raced and I was scared of every noise. I should have pulled off like he told me, but how could I leave him there on a dark isolated road with no way to identify his attacker and possibly later his body. I can't believe Able has sunk to this level; he needs help and fast, because I'm out of here. Until he's ready for us, I'm not ready for this. I should have run for my life at that moment. If that wasn't a defining moment for him I didn't know what would be. After that episode, Able promised never to do that again, endangering my life because his mind was so fogged. Silly me, being the concerned wife, I really saw this as a changing point, boy was I ever wrong. Then I began to reason why should it

131

be a defining moment for him when it wasn't a defining moment for me.

I am no different than Able in my wavering thoughts and actions that's when I realized what I've exclaimed to him many times before that your mouth can and will say anything according to the circumstances you find yourself in. That's the point of our existence, we all would like people to behave accordingly, but remembering that each of us are individuals with our own mind and the way I address my issues will not be the way Able addresses his. From that incident, Able kept his word for a whopping four weeks, and then off to the races again. After that, he was gone from the house for three months at my request. I thought for sure this absence would make his heart grow fonder, bologna. This move would cost me any chances I had of helping my husband. The only thing I accomplished was adding fuel to the fire.

Cain moved in with his sister, Jezzy, the all day in and out weed head. She suggested to me that weed is a better alternative to crack, and maybe Able should try that. Not only did she encourage Cain to change his drug of choice she offered me the drug to supposedly calm my nerves and accept my husbands destructive path; she said it would make it easier for me to deal with. Why a drowning man would begin smoking weed at the age of forty is beyond my comprehension? Who in their right mind would believe weed, crack or any other mind altering substance would be necessary to function.

Candice and I discussed many times how a person's worst enemy could be their family. Candice recalls being her sons worst enemy in the beginning of his addiction, because she would allow him to use her home as a flop house and burger joint; he would be missing for days and then show up dirty, drained, and starving. She reasoned with herself that not letting him in would send him back to the streets, she was afraid to turn him away. I recognized that feeling oh so well. She like me had to learn how to deny him access to those comforts without pushing him away for good. She encouraged me to set limits and stick by them; never in my own strength could I hold fast to the implementing of such tough love without constant prayer and meditation. It reminded me of a movie I saw, in order for the woman to hold on to her sanity she had to light incense and chant. I didn't chant but I prayed for help and guidance.

I started out just lounging around reading and writing trying to enjoy the peace and quiet; trying to keep my hands around my heart to keep it in my chest and all was going well until, yes until the quietness unleashed a storm of tears. I began to sulk and feel sorry for myself again, because I had not set the limits and stuck to them during our young marriage.

I specifically outlined how I felt about his addiction and what I would do if that problem reared its ugly head. I promised him and myself that I would not stick around for any drug usage although he adamantly denied using drugs, but my suspicions lead me to believe otherwise. As I see it, Cain is using and I am still making myself available to him. I have to set limits now even more so because he knows my words have proven not to be my bond. So here are my new limits, no, let me not do that yet until I'm sure of my strength. Well this is what I think will work:
1. Limit my questions to health matters, how are you doing? Then encourage him to pray.
2. Is there anything you need? Then remind him that prayer changes things.

3. Is there anything I can do to help you? Then remind him that God is able to bind up a tormented soul when no one else can.

I think by keeping my questions simple will not compel him to tell lies and both our stress levels will go down. When he asks me questions, I will keep it to the point and not encourage him by lingering in idle chit-chat.

Chapter 23

My mind has always wanted to be strong, but my body kept me down and out until I set these limits at which time I noticed a change in my mood and attitude. Once I started getting out and keeping a full and active schedule his reaction and language changed as if to say he couldn't believe I was doing things without him. My grandmother and aunts would say little things when I was blossoming, one was never let a man see you sweat or cry, but I didn't grasp the meaning, but as a young girl, how could I. The begging and crying I did only make Cain believe he was in control, so when I began to venture out he was forced to analyze how we as individuals operate and the circles we move in.

Moving again was my dose of better, go figure, Able began to call more often; his voice had an air of soundness, and his thoughts were that of concern. The yelling and rage were silent, even if, only for the moment. I concluded that it is a welcomed change any time veins are not popping out of your head when you are talking. Later this evening, tomorrow, or next week things may change but for now the temporary enjoyment of normalcy is all I can cherish.

The generational matriarchs' would say a house is not a home when emptiness is within the walls. I know for a fact the walls of our home were never empty because my heart and soul dwelled there. My address may have changed since hurricane Katrina, but my heart and soul never left me, and any house I reside in will be a home whether or not Able is there. The aftermath of this hurricane seized my things but not my mind; therefore, my goal has remained the same despite being homeless. I've always made sure where my family laid their heads at night was filled with all the love and warmth that I had within me.

I am truly beginning to see the benefit of standing guard over my heart and soul in regards to male and female relationships. My husband and Lauren are currently in an emotional and psychological relationship with each other, no matter how the cookie crumbles, the picture is what the picture is; the unfortunate part about this happens to be in my Able's mind. He honestly sees nothing wrong with the train wreck being mastered over his mind; their child is her trump card and she is directing the train.

It's easy for onlookers to say give Able an ultimatum, but how would that work when his child is and should be his number one priority. The stance I take is a personal one, because as I have sat back and evaluated this particular situation I realize that the child needs him. I know from firsthand experience spouses come and go more often than not these days. The only thing I can say with certainty is that if we are not meant to be for the rest of our lifetime that we part amicably, and if we can't get along, get gone, that's what I feel. This business of human relationships is serious; at almost forty, I have yet to diagram the success of individual personalities coming together from any particular race, background, or class. Our situations and circumstances can change an entire family and it shouldn't be that way, but it is. Many families that appear to be rock solid today prove to be cancerous masses the next day with the ending of marriages and sometimes life.

I would not want my family to be shroud in hidden secrets under any circumstances. I have never been good at keeping secrets, because I am a talker and eventually a secret may slip unless it's my mother's secret or my children's. You know the old saying; *you can't hold sweet water,* that's me. I would assume that everyone is familiar with a situation, and before I realize it, your business is out in the open. When families break apart, accusations fly, feelings get hurt, people have their own opinions about who caused the break up, what happened, and why this family didn't make it. When outsiders can't get the answers to questions that are really none of their business, they make up things, and as a last resort they blame it on the devil and how busy he's been.

Able's calls are all at his whim I don't miss his identifiable ringtone that Motown classic *Love Don't Live Here Anymore.* I dread the calls, some days it's between five and eight calls others it's none this behavior is not my man's. This further fuels my speculations of substance abuse, because I remember a time when Able would not go an hour without wanting to hear from me. Sometimes the unanswered calls result in panic stricken voicemails irrational and loathsome.

Able and I once talked about coming full circle, is that a good or bad thing? I ask myself that all the time, maybe it was the novelty of what's old is new again, maybe it was the sudden loneliness after divorce but whatever the case I wanted and loved this man and he claimed the same thing so when his routine began to change I began to question all the things I've done and he had said. So I had to let Able know how sporadic his mental state had become, and that I had to stop him from calling all together, because his up and down, in and out wishy-washy temperaments were for the birds and this nightingale was fed up.

For every twenty-four hours it gets easier and men sense when their back-bone is backing out. These days I am actually praying for him not to call. If he doesn't call I would fully understand the picture he is trying to paint. His desire is either drugs or Lauren and at this point I can't put my finger on it, but soon, very soon it will reveal itself to me. It would be better for all of us if Able would just tell the truth. Let me make an informed decision based on the truth, is it the woman or drugs simple as that. Not knowing for a certainty has me stuck.

My mother the strongest woman I know has withstood circumstances and situations during her lifetime that should have caused the breakdown of her mental state long time ago including putting up with me through my relationships. She thinks Able is afraid of losing me forever.

So instead of standing up and being accountable he runs and hide from me for fear the truth will permanently shut me out of his life. I am his lifeline; the only person Able knows would move heaven and earth to see him be a better man. My friends-associates say the same thing just not as reserved as my mother. My enemies say that I should have left "Ned", Able where I found him. He is frightened to tell me the truth, but I can hold up under disappointing circumstances more than

138

most people my age, because I have seen and dealt
with a lot of things in my lifetime. If he doesn't
wake up soon this will be the last chapter for us.

Able's people do not care, because they do
not know what love is. Lasting relationships are
not in their history, and unconditional love
escapes their understanding. Unfortunately, it is
something they may never realize for themselves,
so they doubt my love, passion and determination
to give their brother something new and better,
they are envious. In Able's mind, he is not
deserving of all the things I am giving and
showing him, and for years I have watched him deny
himself the pleasurable feeling of recovery. Just
from talking with others I gather Able gets an
instant high or thrill out of being high and
recounting how he is in control of the streets
when he's using, how he rules the world, how he is
the master over his fate. Able's family lingers in
his acts of drug induced ranting and ravings
making fun of his stupidity and mocking his
inability to control his mind. The other addicts
in his family see it as a game and not for the
serious nature it is. He could die from this
addiction. Where is the common sense in all this
madness? It's not good to judge a book by its
cover but I'm speaking from eyewitness accounts of
the things I've seen and heard, too many to count
and some too frightening to think about, this
family ordeal has blown my mind.

When I think about Lauren and her situation
it scares me to think I could end up like her
always having to play second fiddle, the runner
up. This can easily happen if I start a pattern of
allowing Able to bring his destructive ego Cain
into my life and what is supposed to be our
private space. In Lauren's case I tend to see her
frustration in that there was the first Mrs. and
now me. In those years unknown to me Able lived

139

with her and they produced a child and never once has she found a place in his life as number one. Their life together had no real substance according to her, and I'm sure Able sensed the disconnection between them.

When their child was born Lauren's opportunity increased to solidify Able's commitment to his seed. Even with the birth of their daughter, Lauren never sealed Able's heart. Before we married I personally committed myself to including her into our lives for the sake of harmony. Then when my man was down she thought her vices would win, so now I despise her want of heart. Lauren has said and did everything she thought possible to cause friction within my family. Her vicious and unwarranted attacks on my character have pushed me to that point. The point of viewing her as the kid in the contest at school, and although she may have put her best foot forward for some reason she cannot manage a first place trophy, a second place metal, or a third place certificate the most she ever gets is an honorable mention ribbon. Lauren will never receive first place in this competition against me. The worst that can happen is I will become widowed and their child will miss the presence of her father as she grows into a woman.

Now that Able and I are facing some differences of opinion she feels as if she is sitting on top of my world, but in all actuality it's not Able who is using her it's Cain. His need for her attention is out of pure desperation, and I have expressed to both of them that they should be ashamed of themselves for enabling each other to wallow in the others misery. Her crash and his fall will be harder the second time around when she realizes that she hasn't placed again in this game that she is playing. What's more pathetic than always being over looked? Any other day of the week, these two would be made for each other, it just so happens he in all his woes belongs to yet another woman other than her, and that woman happens to be me.

Able is a gem although it's hard to see at this moment, maybe I need my head examined, but I love him and the love I have for Able cannot be replaced with a temporary shelter made of paper thin lies. Cain is diseased there is a massive layer of abnormal matter coating his ability to think. It's hard even for me to imagine some of the things he says and does. Lauren could realize the gem in Able too, but she is so scared that he will not love her in sobriety that she welcomes him in this sickened state. I see this man as the strong backbone he could be and any woman would desire so why let him fall if there is any way possible to help him stand. Lauren and Able both were motherless children although her mother was alive in the physical sense she lead a life clouded with addiction, and her father neglected her and her siblings. I'm not sure as to all the circumstances surrounding her childhood but Able often spoke of her not having anyone to rely on but herself. Her need for Able in this condition is sad, but what can I say about this woman whose goal is to have him back under her wings as a crack addicted man with no sense of purpose or direction. I guess it's time for me to accept the fact that this is the life he wants to live. Lauren must have a reward of some sort knowing that he will always run to her as his last ditch to lie in. At this point, I can only feel for the child who is innocent and whose parents are living a lie. Lauren's heart will always wonder if Able will ever place her as number one. I have and still am number one too many admirers past and present; however, I chose Able and now I am wondering if and when he will allow me the honesty I deserve.

141

Maybe one day I'll sit back and write a book without all the twist and turns that hurt instead, of heal. Dear Comforter, life-giver and strength, I am finally moving on today, I called Able for the last time and proclaimed my love; however, I am no longer going to be his punching bag. This reality hurts, this life I am living stinks. Thinking about my lowest point scares me to death. The weakness of my mind is troubled, perplexed, and unruly. I in my insanity allowed the utterance of a mad woman stricken with suicidal thoughts to speak of giving up, quitting and ending my own life. I no longer need a love like this; I no longer want a love like this when I gave my power there was nothing left for me. With the power I relinquished I no longer possessed my trained, spirited God given mind. How did I ever contemplate ending my life, the gift that God gives, because of Cain's ruthlessness? The things I know oh so well I lost somewhere down this road over the past year. I allowed Cain to become my thorn and I'm just recognizing how deeply my soul is wounded. Wanting to die is not the thoughts of a once vibrant and stable woman, only people suffering from some sort of mental illness could ever consider this as their only way out of a bad situation, I know better. I've known better all of my life; my mother raised a self-confident resilient woman and this is so unlike me. Being strong has always been a part of my fiber when things go wrong, and when things go right my phone is the first to ring. Everyone wants to share their news with me, and how or why I have allowed this negative spirit to consume my mental capacity to reason is something I need to search out.

Chapter 24

Thinking about how I let the words, *I feel like dying,* cross my lips, and then escape out of my mouth is disheartening to me. I grew up knowing that sticks and stones might break my bones but words cannot hurt me. I'm fortunate to be alive; for reasons unknown to me I have allowed my life to revolve around this man and his craziness. If he wants to throw his life away I'm going to step aside, even though, I know my presence is needed and wanted. His addiction has driven me to the edge and what for? I cannot fall into the trap laid for me; the pit is open, but I'm not the one entering. I followed my wayward heart and diseased mind for far too long in dealing with this madness, it's high time I reclaim and resume my pre-Katrina mind, the same one that lead me to safety. The mind I lost for my first love, denied by my second love, and will use in all future loves. There should not be pain associated with a real love for self if balanced with dignity. The respect I gave to Able when I first allowed the signs and symptoms of his addiction to go unchecked by being his counselor instead of remaining his wife has perpetrated this lie. I knew full well even the best minds are defeated by a person's strong will to stay in denial. Because admitting he had a problem would mean he was denying help. I will walk alone for awhile; I'll shed tears. I'll have sleepless nights; I will miss him. I will want him, but I will not regret my choice to move forward. I will stand up; I will call out his name in sheer want, or I will want to hold his hand, but I will not give in to his denial and self pity anymore. I will see blue skies and rainbows without him; I will travel to distant places without my Able. I will laugh again without him, but I will not lie down and die because of him. I have made it through tougher situations; I have seen greater tragedy and lived to tell the story.

This is me hurt, crushed, shattered, and forever changed by my own hands; I allowed this transformation, and there is no one else to blame. I have so much left to give myself and my family that I do not have time to sit and weep over things that I cannot change, even if I could, would this have made me a better person?

My children need their mother healthy and strong, and my mother needs to see her daughter's happiness once again. My mother mentioned to me how she has witnessed my sadness even when I thought I was happy that revelation coming from her silenced me, for I had now known the extent to which I could not cover my anguished disposition. The world is iced over without your mother, so I plan on sticking around for my crew regardless of how my relationship may or may not work out with this man. If the devil's goal for me is death, I have a fight on my hands and so does he, because as a child of God I am loved, blessed and protected from the blows. The time to acknowledge my defeat has not arrived, but when it does Able and everyone else involved will know that I am still standing, taller and stronger than ever before. The prayer says I fear you not.

Right now I want to focus on conquering the emotional upheaval in my life, because I have been down for too long hoping that someone or something would come and rescue me, but there was no rescue team for my broken heart. The help I required would have to come from the depth of my soul. I had to be the one to decide when and how to mend my broken heart. Why must I mend my broken heart? Good question, but one that escaped my mind when I again let down my guard and allowed Able into my bosom.

My stronger mind suggested we meet in a public place, but my weaker desire for his touch lead me to his arms in a remote corner suite that had all the modern amenities that I needed to indulge myself with a little music, some wine and my toys, but nothing could replace the touch of my Able. All I could see and feel was the fire of touch; the trembling of his hands as he embraced me for the first time in months, the tears. There were the warm tears streaming down my face, which prompted my Able to affectionately kiss them away, as only he could. We struggled for a few moments, but I wanted to savor this time in my feminine psyche while Able wanted me in his masculine power; we both missed the chemistry we so often shared. He softly uttered love notes in my ear, as if, singing the sweetest song I had ever heard. He whispered I love you. This scared me because I had not heard him say those words to me in three days, but it didn't stop the energy that was flowing through the room; it did give me a glimmer of light in my darkest journey in adult love. I knew why I had requested a secluded suite; I wanted Able to make love to me as only he could. Our absence from each other fueled a sexual encounter that was swift, sweaty and satisfying. Able buried

145

his head, I covered my mouth, he unleashed his pallet, my mouth opened, my eyes widened, and my upper torso rose; only to be laid down with the gentle force of his strong hands. The stroke of his Lamina left me gasping for air; with everything in me I tried to call his name but it eluded me. I was held captive by my own weakness as my body was strictly under his control.

This is our downfall we make the notes together in sync with one another at a time and place that we share in secret. As with any great work, making the notes are only the beginning, and with every beat you add clarity, but now that I have allowed myself to fall back ten steps emotionally, where do I go from here? Do I say what needs to be said? Do I ask the questions that will divide my spirit? When I am really thinking, girl, just enjoy the moment. Enjoying the moment for me has a totally different meaning for Able; he thinks all is forgiven when I'm thinking about the next round being on me for me. My sexuality is what has me at a crossroad with my mind, and right now my desire is to take it down a notch only to escalate the intensity, because that's the way I operate when it comes to pleasing me; I don't know when the next time I'll feel his touch, so let me.

I take no prisoners just captives; Able is my target of ecstasy. I love the way he tastes, the sweet saltiness of his muscular organ locked to my lips, and the back of his neck when I begin to fondle him, gently with meticulous strokes of my tongue, my journey to his spot is slow and precise, caressing, nibbling, sucking all with the great passion that I feel for my man. His moans are beastlike, his thunderous thighs caramel brown... uh, uh. Uh is where I sit and wait for his up and down advances that initiate one of those inferior orgasms. The strength in his legs is enormous as he lifts me up without any effort.

146

I enjoy the ride. I straddle the gun arranging my legs securely so I can, and trust me I will not lose ground. The feeling of my man inside my secret earth is indescribable. Not that he is overly blessed with his package but when I go there it's out of love, and there is nothing I will not do for the man I love, because I still feel like he is the only one for me. Maybe not the right only but you get my drift.

I let all my guards down when we are together, and I know I shouldn't but for the moment I place it out of my mind. He allows me to be myself in expressing my fantasies. The ride is almost over, so I make a sudden slide to his breast, his spot, so that I can power up his erection, because I love to hear him whimper. It energizes me, catapulting me into instant and forceful gyrations that cause us both to climax, game, set, match and I'm finished; he's finished and my Able understands my routine. Don't touch me; I'm coming down off my high, and all I can utter is thank you, thank you, thank you, mission accomplished. The sexual nature of our relationship is one envied by lonely housewives who have yet to experience anything outside of missionary formation.

I am still skeptical about everything now, but I do not regret spending time with my Able it was great the laughs, the passion, the walks; however, the harsh reality is that it does not remove the sting of betrayal by him, the fact that he has sacrificed our home, the sacredness and the security of our bed, and our marriage not to mention the precious lives of our children. I am not alone in my struggle; I am not weak in my knowledge, and I have to admit that I am terrified of this uncertainty in my heart. My girlfriends would be the first to tell you that I always ask what he does for you standing up. Because we all know how a man, your man, can make you feel lying down.

Right now all I can do is reminisce about the time when my Able would stand up against any force that threatened to harm me. There was a certain cockiness he possessed and the commanding way he walked made a statement loud and clear even before he uttered a sound. It scares me to imagine how disrespectful I've heard the streets can be, because no one knows your name when you're smoking dope, getting high. Able lost his standing with me months ago; I do not feel safe in his life anymore, and he's not safe in his life anymore. He cried on my shoulder the other night pouring out his aching heart, his troubled mind, and broken spirit. The tears he cried were those of a prisoner with no way out. I held him in my arms and prayed for him while asking God to remove this obstacle from my husband, from my friend, from my man. No one feels a man's tears more than his mother or his wife.

We are gutted with anguish. Able and I both need prayer at this point. How long can I see him like this? How much more can I take? How can we find the light at the end of this cold and dark tunnel? I personally hate it here the daily uncertainty, vulgar thoughts, crippling zeal, and diminished dreams. This disease is slowly and agonizingly killing my spirit and my prayers for sanity are constant. I cannot make this thing go away. The best advice is not good enough and the worst advice has not changed anything; Able has to get tired, he has to bottom out, and the saddest part of this entire ordeal is that he is aware of the outcome.

This man feels trapped by his own weakness, and for every forward stride there is a vicious sliding back at the hands of everyone around him,

148

his family, the streets, and himself; Able's personal admissions speak volumes. He has admitted how his sister, Jezzy, is cold and calculating, and that her back stabbing was harmful. But his love for her blinds him to the knife that she has plunged into his back, and the constant steady attempts to puncture his heart. He has admitted how his brothers are rotten, his cousins are poisonous, but he cannot shake what he hungers for still, their love. I felt the pounding of his heart, and the blood pumping through valves as he wept telling me the stories I have heard time and time again about his desire to be loved by his family, and how he envies my relationship with my mother because he never experienced that kind of love. The words I say are not enough; the things I do only temporarily mask the real problem. I know there is really nothing I can do or say to take away his pain, except, I am sorry honey that I have failed you, because I am at a lost for answers or a cure.

My husband is in a crisis and no one other than me cares enough to consider getting him help. He is yelling for a life vest, and the people he believes love him are on the shore, hiding the vest behind their backs, under their feet, and in their misery I hate them all. Able's mind is not being controlled by the rational man that is deep within him; it's warped by the drug, and he is crying out for an intervention. I asked Cain yesterday if he would prefer I throw in the towel on him and this relationship, to leave him alone in his addiction, and again he forcefully denied his sickness is alive and active in our lives. I again asked him what he wants me to do for him, and he begged me to be patient because he is lost. He asked me not give up on him, and pleaded for my heart not to become obstinate. I'm thinking just pack up and abandon this sinking ship, but my first mind says to leave this massive hell right now. Able's not the only one plagued with addiction. I've had a few family members and friends who were in decade long addictions go into recovery. I have a very dear and close friend who is fifteen years strong in her recovery process so I know there is hope.

Chapter 25

The environment that Able has chosen to dwell and work in is drug infested; the air is polluted because everyone he is in association with uses some illegal narcotic, chemically harmful to their body and mind. They alter their minds every day. Able's first step toward recovery would be to distance himself and seek a treatment program, and then make a earnest effort to plan the work he has before him and work his plan. Staying clean and sober is easiest said by the person not in addiction. Being an addict leaves little to no room for playful meetings of chance. Able has to grow in his understanding of flirtation. Crossing paths with a former pusher or smoking buddy maybe inevitable but what is the proper protocol. I say he should speak and keep moving; he on the other hand seems to think he is bigger than his addiction shaking hands, smiling, dapping each other while exchanging numbers all lead to something more, relapse. Avoiding intimate interactions are a must to remaining in recovery that's my unprofessional wife opinion.

Last week during a temporary stint of
soberness Able and I discussed the various forms
of addictions that people have and how their plan
for sober living include reconditioning their
entire outlook on life. The unsafe environments in
which you live, work, and play as well as the
people we associate with. I shared personal
details of my experience with what I thought was
an addiction. Some years back I was seeking help
for what I thought was a sex addiction after
attending several meetings and consulting with a
licensed professional it was concluded that I came
nowhere close to being labeled a sex addict. The
fact that I enjoy physical touch and intimacy with
my partner disqualified me as an addict. My
desires and fantasies do not drift to include
others, which is a real indicator of the value
I've placed on our marriage.I explained this to
Able and he seemed shocked that I would still
choose to want him in his confused state but I
understand fear.

I am addicted to him and I admittedly need
help for my problem. I think Able and I are both
experiencing some sort of madness in our lives. I
know other couples are also going through motions
in their relationships. It's unfortunate that no
one can really give you an answer because they are
dealing with their own problems. Even if someone
thought they had the answer, what works for one
relationship may not work for another even if
they're in the same situation because of the
different personalities. The more I sit and think
the sadder I become over Able's dilemma, because
he is not the same man and I have definitely
changed, and maybe it's time we go our separate
ways for good. Something is holding me back; I
can't let go and for some reason he won't let go.
This fatal yearning has caused me my sanity; we
both can't afford this tragic outcome.

152

Able denies everything in his life that has caused his depression. His therapist says the new medication could have triggered these short term binges. I have never heard of such a thing as short term binges until now, but I guess that is what experts' call thirty days sober two days drugging, one hundred and twenty days sober, forty-eight hours drugging. The mad man Cain is in my thoughts constantly. I'm afraid to sleep for fear I may wake up, and scared to wake up for fear of falling asleep; I know it's crazy but that's where I am. I have had it up to my eyeballs in disappointment, but I steadily go back for more, and now the momentary pleasure that I get from lying down with him is minimized by the dramatic outburst that I know will surface when things don't go his way. The sadness in his eyes was overwhelming when I dropped him off at Lauren's house last night. I pulled to the side of an under lit roadway and sobbed because I miss Able.

Book Club Notes

Chapter 26

The shell of Cain is empty beyond what I'm used to seeing his small frame, fifty pounds lighter, unshaved, eyes bulging, and reeking of the streets. It's like this addiction has sanded the insides of his brain cavity leaving an abrasive residue for the next person to clean. I guess that person will be Lauren; all I could do was hold him close to my overly nervous heart while rubbing his head and whispering in his ear, *Able you can get better help is available.* When he called earlier in his muffled voice, I knew it was him, Able. Cain never speaks with a sober tongue; his voice is always heavy and dragging. Able, however, is remorseful that's how I distinguish between the two.

He finally admitted what I had predicted all along that his addiction to crack would take a toll on his ability to make good decisions. Cain's lack of control endangered his child and exposed her to the vicious lifestyle of an addict. Able acted as if Lauren would mind and wanted me there when he confessed the outrageous level to which he had sunk. Able said to Lauren, *I have something to tell you and it's real bad.* Lauren answered, *what is it?*

You know I have been getting high and for the past two days I took the baby with me to score and smoke crack. She didn't see me, because I left her in the other room with Jezzy.

Lauren said, *why did you do that? I don't know* Cain replied. Lauren asked him if he was going to do that again.

Lauren, please help me beat this addiction by letting me go; I know you're sick and the baby needs me but I have a family. I love my wife and I'm a better person when Liz and I are together.

You are so stupid; Able you are what you are, a dope fiend, and crack head and being with her rather than our daughter is proof that you are incompetent. I love you; I love you for who you are, and not what you want to be.

I had heard it all; I politely excused myself from my car, because this triangle was like dangling over a live wire with a sea of water underneath. I honestly don't know why he needed me there as he pleaded with Lauren for her to cut him loose. He was begging the mother of his child to stop enabling his sickness, ridiculous.

What I experienced is the making of a cartoon with all the sound effects and

unbelievable resurrections possible. Why Cain
couldn't tell Lauren face to face without me
there? What is my connection to their secrets? I
can only assume Lauren is a user and burning both
ends of a candle at the same time is not a wise
move. I'm sad about how I feel caught in the
middle, and I need closure, because these secret
rendezvous are only pacifying the underlying
issues. A friend once told me there is no sense in
being in love by yourself; I am seeing the wisdom
in those words. She mentioned how loving and
wanting to fix what I didn't break is impossible,
and if I can't truly forgive him for what I feel
in my heart of hearts that he has done than it
will only hurt longer if I keep him around, how
true. I know what she has said is real because I
feel this way myself, but the question still
remains within me, what am I going to do about
this? I am the only one on the losing end, and
everybody else seems to be getting what they want,
so maybe it's better this way. Leaving this
relationship with my memories is better than
leaving it in a pine box. Since Able has branded a
still and cold distrust on my heart, I'm reminded
that those better times will never come again in
my lifetime; this is heartbreaking to me.

After having sex with my love, I feel empty,
violated, because I honestly feel that his touch
is no longer sacred. That secret place we shared
has been victimized, our bodies, his body doesn't
feel, taste, or smell the same. Before this
situation with Lauren, I always wanted to please
him, but I don't feel the same. No matter what he
says I feel as though I'm sharing him, and I'm not
good at sharing my man. I wish this doubt could be
laid to rest but I'm not sure it can be. I love
him and I miss him; those two things will never
change. I think about the other woman and I know
her wanting him will never change. There is
nothing anyone of us can do to change the others

desire. Haunted, disappointed and scared, I think every time we are together is our last so I try to prepare myself by offering him a way out. He can't say it on his own, because his denial of his drug induced relationship is just like his denial in admitting his reoccurring addiction.

Keeping my head up is getting harder. If I continue in this way I am going to break, and who needs or wants a broken woman and mother. His eyes say he wants and needs me but his mind is in a tug of war with his heart; he can't make any rational decisions from this crooked path he is blindly following. Nothing offers him any escape from this madness. This morning I woke up and Able was sleeping, resting peacefully; he slept well under his security blanket, me. He opened his eyes and wanted to venture into my secret place, but this morning was different I denied him access. I didn't want to leave feeling used; although, I have been playing myself cheap for some time now. His co-dependent wife had left the room; it was time to return back to reality. He was going north into his dark secrets, and I was headed south in more ways than one. As I moved toward the edge of the bed, I thought about the spectacular love making we had engaged in during the past forty-eight hours, and I guess he was still reeling from it also. Able grabbed me and said, *please don't leave me like this, I want your scent, I crave your depth, I need your touch*. Without putting up much of a fight I allowed him to penetrate my heart as he pierced my inner walls, he fondled my clit with his sword and went as deep as his muscle would allow. I know the power of his suction, the flaring of his nostrils, the growl of his vocal cord, he hungered for ecstasy, and I gave him the motion he was searching for up and down, round and round. I even gave him hot and cold with the ice cubes that numb my insides so that I sit at attention until the heat melts the cubes, and the

cool water quenches his thirst. Then I am at ease,
knowing that no other female would delight in
making Able's fantasies come true like me. He
comes up for air, nose sweaty, mouth watering,
eyes wide and bright with gratitude for allowing
him to take me there. In his mind, he has won me
over again and for awhile I guess he has. After
searching and finding my secret, Able kisses me
and I agree without conversation to complete the
session; I open his eyes with the soft and gentle
nibbles that only my lips know how to give, and I
invite him to watch me as I engage in sensual
foreplay tasting the tips of his fingers. With the
honey drippings from my Excellency, he pants and
wants to touch but I fight him off playfully. I
ride his Johnson as if I was on the motor speedway
making swift turns, accelerating then breaking
without fore thought, hoping to see the finish
line but not wanting to cross. I just love this
man who allows me to be free in my expressions of
human sexuality. There is no other man I would
rather be with than my Able. I am lost in my own
desires, trapped in my own mind, and forgotten by
my lover's heart. I am the one in denial I need a
healing from my *addiction* to him. It's mind
boggling to me how I refuse to escape.

This is the last time I will meet him on his
terms. I have had enough of this paper chase. It's
even crazier what happens after the relapse that
got me thinking can this man be serious? Cain does
this thing where he calls to ask if he can come
home. Oddly enough he didn't get my permission to
leave why would he need it now? I tell him the
door that you walked out of as a sober man is the
same door, it hasn't changed; you've changed! Cain
is hostile as usual telling me about my sarcasms.
Waking me out of a sound sleep, hell I was
comfortable. He came into the house; no longer our
home, because his addiction destroyed that months
ago. Cain was silent for a few moments; I guess he

159

sensed the calmness in me, and was scared to utter a sound. He looked for the panic, but I gave him no satisfaction at the moment he expected. This time it was different, he had all those stupid questions like do you want me to go? Do you still love me? Do you want me? And then he started with the stupid whys. I don't know why I turned that block. I don't know what happened to me. I don't know why Jezzy offered me a freebie. I don't know why I messed up. Why me? I told him in a soft whisper to do what he wants. I wasn't in a position to make anymore decisions for him, it was strictly up to him whether he would stay or leave. It took everything in me to hold my peace. Messing up is Cain's favorite words, it's not messing up, the correct wording would be I smoked crack again. Not to mention or acknowledge that he left out the house with a *grand* in his pocket, squandering a week's pay, and looking absurd; the house had needs that week, and now I will have to supply those needs. I couldn't help but think he's so stupid!

He sat at the foot of our bed; the one we had passionately made love on just twelve hours earlier and asked me to pray. *Lord,* I could have flipped my wig but I didn't. I told Cain he needed to ask God to help him first before we could pray together. In my mind I'm thinking, why not pray before you smoke the crack. It takes a lot more effort to hustle the dope, find a spot to smoke it, and then duck the paranoia, than it would have taken you a few seconds to pray for a way out.

Cain always wants to sex his way to forgiveness but not tonight. I remember that last time he went on a spree and came home with *crabs*; I always think about the next time, it could be worst. Out there in the streets going from crack house to crack house you can pick up on anything. I told him to lie down and get some rest. He

160

crawled to the bed; I politely got up and made him a pallet on the floor. I surprised myself and thought, I am okay; it's just a matter of time before I walk away. Cain tossed and turned feverishly the rest of the night until his alarm went off. He bounced up and fell into his routine of getting ready for work. I am astonished to say the least that he can continue to operate; that is until he is under the influence of cocaine. While getting dressed he woke me up but this time I wasn't so calm; here he comes with the begging for my money. This dope fiend went out smoked his money and don't have gas in his ride. Now he has my attention. Cain is an ass! So he said, *I need money,* the worst thing you can say after a drug binge. Those words pierce my soul; it's the same as adultery to me, staying out all night with something other than me glued to your lips. Didn't he know that he would need gas and lunch money for the week ahead. Boy, I let out a piercing scream; Cain rustled to reach the front door because he knew my venom was about to disable him. I am afraid to open my mouth for fear of the truth coming out. I don't know the truth from lies anymore. Cain uses our marital commitment as a basis for me to keep quiet about his transgressions. I ask Cain what's the difference between telling the truth and telling a lie he says *crack*, he admits that he has never wanted to lie to me, but once he smokes he knows I won't understand the truth. I say the difference is love. Love is not inherited, it's cultivated; I cultivated a love for him that he has yet to cultivate for himself. How can I expect him to love me enough not to lie when he is constantly lying to Able? His life is being snuffed out slowly by the only person alive to save him, and that's himself. Truly there must be an end to the wavering of both our minds. Yet again, Cain got into his automobile and sped away; a few minutes later he called apologizing for not being true to me. I am not the one who needed his acceptance, that's personal, and to date he still wants mans approval for his addiction related mistakes.

Yesterday was wonderful while today is full of disappointment. I'm not making it any better. I am on my own tidal wave, trying to ride it.

Chapter 27

One spring when Cain was on the run, I met Marvin in Miami. Umm… he came up to my girlfriend Liza an asked my name. Liza being a jokester tried to discourage this specimen of a man from wanting to meet me; however, he had an agenda. From what I could see, there were some spectacular views of abs, biceps, triceps, and hamstrings; I thought to myself, wow! You know the kind you would expect to see with all those fine youngsters attending that annual beach party in Florida. My girls forced me to the south end of Florida to get my mind off Able. Liza told Marvin that I was married with two sons, and that he could have more fun with her than with little old me. He said the view he relished was of the married one and that I couldn't possibly be married wearing that bathing suit so well.

Reluctantly Liza guided him to me, and all I could say was *laud have mercy on me.* Marvin was definitely my type, tall, about six three, dark and toting a *six pack.* I had seen him pass by a few times but had no idea he was scoping me out. He introduced himself, and I was like that naïve

163

school girl Able knew, and still acting like I didn't recognize a pick up line. Liza had to interject *I told you my girl is not for you, I am!* Marvin turned his attention back to me saying *don't be shy, what's your name?* With an air of agitation, I replied, *Mrs. Able!* Marvin said he didn't want to disturb us but if he passed by one more time without speaking he was going to regret not knowing my name. I said, *well there you have it, Mrs. Able married to Mr. Able, and you have a wonderful rest of the day.* Liza jumped her messy ass in and invited this stranger to buy us drinks; Liza is just that kind of girl, boisterous but never meaning any harm.

He was glad to oblige her demand ordering us a round of drinks. I requested a non-alcoholic drink; Liza brought me back a shot of the old gentlemen she knows, but I didn't need a drink without my man around to finish my intoxication. Marvin said he would like to have us over for an early dinner; he didn't want to miss the fireworks, this being the last night of the weekend's events. Liza and I sat around the beach for another hour or so then we headed back to the condo to freshen up. I was considered the maternal one in our little clique mainly because I knew how to behave.

I started to doubt whether or not we should have dinner with this man, because I could feel attraction towards him but Liza was excited to be joining Marvin for dinner especially since he said that he would introduce her to a few of his friends. I was ready to leave when Liza said, *I know you are not wearing that old grandma sookie dress;* I replied to her, *why not?*

Liz you are going way too far to the other side, earlier on the beach you wore

164

that two-piece that made you look twenty-one now you look...

I stopped her in her tracks,

What exactly do I look like Liza, my age, forty? Unlike some people Liza, looking and acting mature is what makes me sexier. It was my quiet sophistication that led Marvin to ask you my name!

Okay Liz you don't have to beat me up with words, I can't stand when you're right. Shoot, you are the only married woman in our circle and the men always flock your way. They always want to know who you are; well, I guess you know a little something-something.

Are you ready Liza? Yes. As we were about to leave, there was a knock at the door, but by time I looked through the peep hole there was nobody there. Liza opened the door, and there was a gorgeous floral arrangement at her feet. She reached down to grab the vase and the note attached said Mrs. Able, Orchids and Magnolias are for southern bells. Liza was ecstatic until she realized the gift wasn't meant for her. *Girl this mess is for you, come on we're going to be late,* she smirkingly said. Liza was steaming as we exited the room. I was nervous about the entire evening not knowing what to expect, or how I would react to being in a room of single men with one of them showing interest in me. We hailed a taxi and headed towards Marvin's rented beach house. The ride was only three city blocks, but it seemed more like a country mile. As we drove up to the

beach house, there were several young men outside
as if to welcome our arrival. Liza was calm, but
my stomach had butterflies; I wanted the taxi to
keep moving, but it didn't. Once it stopped,
Marvin walked to my side of the taxi, opened my
door, reached for my hand, helped me out of the
vehicle, and kissed my cheek. He reminded me of my
Able, sweet, gentle almost too good to be true.
That's what I missed in the latter part of our
relationship, and during his addiction; the sweet
innocence of it all. Liza was escorted by one of
the other young men into the house as Marvin and I
walked slowly with his hand still holding mine. I
knew there was going to be trouble for me if I
didn't put a stop to this gorgeous young man
paying this much attention to me. The other ladies
we had been hanging out with were already at the
dinner table when we walked in. For some reason I
didn't feel out of place. Even as Marvin pulled
out my chair, I was thinking that having dinner
with strange people, so much younger, would make
me feel awkward. I noticed the place was stunning,
it had vaulted ceilings, fifteen feet high, and
the drapes were a beautiful rich mocha with French
blue geometrics, definitely a man space. I had a
few cocktails during dinner, and laughed like I
hadn't laughed in a long time. Marvin had sexiness
about him that I found intriguing. His maturity
was impressive for a young man, the entire evening
we talked about everything from college to family.
He wants to get his Master's in Engineering and
someday be a family man and a good provider. I
agreed with him that those things are important,
long-term goals.

The dinner was fantastic. All the men had
gotten together preparing everything from the
appetizer to the dessert. Marvin said he prepared
and baked the better than sex cake; it was the
best I had ever eaten, particularly, since it was
baked by a man. I thought to myself, he bakes. Who

knew later on I would find out that he could bake
at any temperature. When Marvin rose from the
table, it felt as if my breathing increased. I
knew I liked what I was looking at and that the
chemistry was already there. I have several
philosophies one of them being the law of
attraction initiates conversation, opening the
door to dialogue, leading to information that will
either move you forward or shut you down, this
holds true not only in love but in life. So now
that Marvin and I have engaged each other in
conversation, and I have had a few drinks, not
even I know where this will lead. In my mind I
don't want anything to happen, but in my heart I
want him. It's been eleven months since Able and I
made love. I need it! But, I'm going to act like a
lady. I know if it was Liza she would be undressed
and waiting, but I'm different. I was schooled by
the best; if it weren't for protecting my
children, my chosen profession would be
credentialed *love goddess*. Not even Liza knows of
my capabilities; I just let her go on thinking the
way she thinks. She wonders why I attract men;
it's not always the outside appearance that
attracts the opposite sex. It has more to do with
the mystery in me. I have a hidden sex appeal that
men see in my demeanor.

Marvin walked over to the other side of the
room and pulled the drapes; the patio was amazing,
it was staged to look like a disco lounge with
rolling lights, a wooden floor and a martini bar.
It was already half past twelve and I was just
about ready for bed. Liza and I were going home
the next day on an afternoon flight. I told Marvin
there was no way I could stay, but he asked me not
to leave. I told him we had to go or else we would
miss our flight. I beckoned for Liza as she threw
back jello shots, *I'm not ready to go,* Liza
exclaimed! *Girl you know we have a flight for
twelve.* Liza was adamant about staying and our

167

rule of thumb was if we go together we leave together that's our bond. I pouted for a few minutes because I really was exhausted. Liza never knows when to call it quits.

Marvin sensed my frustration; he just sat next to me without uttering a sound all the while holding my hand. I asked him to get me a drink, by this time I needed a stiff one, no pun intended, maybe a little bit. We walked and talked as I tried to keep an eye on Liza, she was full herself, anyone of those guys could have had their way with her and she wouldn't know it. I have told her a hundred times I can't watch her cat; I have trouble watching my own, and tonight it was heading for trouble. There was a grassy area near the north corner of the house that was lit only by the stars, as Marvin held my hand, I began to subtlety resist. I knew that corner was too dark for us to see anything let alone anyone to see us. He asked me to lie under the stars with him; I said that was not a good idea. He asked, *why*. I told him mainly because I am a married woman or did you conveniently forget. He said no, *I remember you're married, not happily, have wonderful children that you adore, have goals and dreams you have yet to accomplish; I just want to help you relax a bit*. There was silence as he came out of his shirt, placed it on the grass, and laid me down. I was thinking to myself did I subconsciously want this; maybe that's why I wore a dress with no drawers, instead of a pants outfit. I did do my hair a little fancier, and sprayed some of Liza's perfume on the back of my calves. God knows I'm going to be in trouble with him in the morning if he hasn't reserved me for extinction already. Marvin said I made him smile and laugh with my entertaining conversation; he liked the way I seemed to take things in stride.

If you Change the Words
you Change the MEANING

We laid there and whispered sweet nothings in each other's ears, by this time the alcohol kicked in, I reached for the brim of Marvin's boxers easing my hand in to gently stroke his Chinese arithmetic. I was in need and missing the touch of a man. Feeling on Marvin ignited a fire in me that I had tried my hardest to extinguish. Thinking in the front of my mind how to get up and run as fast as my feet would let me and wrestling with the back of my mind to succumb. Both of which were engulfed in the pulsating heat coming from his mouth. For a split second I reasoned in my mind the backlash I would face, and then I let loose of all thoughts. As Marvin forcefully groped my crotch, I sought more; doing everything I could imagine while trying to conceal my intimate screams. Every touch was potent engraving his signature on my body. He kissed my lips as if there was honey dripping from them, as he orchestrated his mighty hands to perform a duet for two. From the nape of my neck to the small of my spine Marvin effortlessly played my tune. I was in expectation of no more. As I attempted to wrap my legs around his back, he gently maneuvered them to the outside of his shoulders. I was wide open relinquishing all my fight. Marvin caressed my inner spirit communicating as if he invented all the intricacies involved in human touch. It was over for me; I felt my orgasm, and Marvin with a soft whisper assured me that it was okay as I lingered in my intense climax. My vocals were bound in guilt, not for the infidelity which I am not convinced I committed, but for the pleasurable emotions that followed both in my mind and body. Within minutes I heard Liza calling for me, by that time I knew we needed to leave. Marvin asked me to stay but I declined, he then drove us back to our condo.

As Liza headed into the foyer, Marvin opened my door, he said we shouldn't let this night end;

169

I however, was journeying back to my life as a married woman in derision still not sure as to my future. I thanked him for the great time. As I turned to walk away he passionately pulled me back into his arms placing my hand to his chest, and asked if I could count the beats. I couldn't because his heart was beating faster than mine; I knew I had to leave but I wanted to stay. I had no intentions of beginning something that would possibly end tragically for either Marvin or I. He gave me his number; kissed me and walked away.

After boarding the plane, Liza began with all her questions about what Marvin and I did, but I assured her that the golden rule applied. We weren't going to discuss what took place in Miami from that moment on. I had no intention of ever seeing him again. I ignored her, eased into a restful position with my head planted against the window and reminisced about my great get away. I nodded off rather quickly; I suppose waking up in a dream. It was Able and I; we had reconciled our differences after he spent more than nine months in a sober living environment. He suggested we start fresh, a part of that new beginning meant that we would relocate. It had to be close enough for him to continue his work but far enough for us to maintain our distance from whatever. I was okay with the move but skeptical of the future. His addiction had cut me deeper than I could ever really put into words. My faith in God softened my heart for one more chance at saving my marriage.

Able and I chose Picayune, Mississippi. The commute was only an hour and a half away from his work and his child. We were doing wonderful, I was doing consulting work from home, he was attending recovery meetings, and we attended counseling as a family. Although, we were together there still was a need for us to mend our marriage. Able had always wanted another child, which seemed absurd, because he wasn't stable enough to love the one he had. Two strong and good years into his recovery we got pregnant and things were going great. I wasn't ready to be a mother again my babies were all in school but as life would have it a bouncing baby girl arrived into our lives. Able promised no more backsliding. I believed him, supported him in every way possible, and then! One day Able called to say he would be a little late, I suspected nothing wrong since he mentioned there was an accident on the high-rise. I began to worry that something dreadful had happened to him on the way in because he wasn't answering his phone. This was very unlike him unless he was using again. My mind began to run in so many directions; it felt like my thoughts were swimming in the head. It was now seven o'clock in the evening, and I had heard nothing. How could he do this to me, to this innocent child of ours, and especially to himself? I was frantically trying to gather my thoughts when Able came through the door with a pretty pink bear and some magnolias. My heart dropped to the floor, exhausted from all the unnecessary worries, *where were you Able, I was in a panic thinking that something happened.* I told you Liz there is nothing to worry about. I put the baby in his arms, walked to the bathroom, locked the door, turned the shower on as hot as I could stand it, and cried.

Liz wake up, we're home, Liza shouted as she shoved my arm. *Girl I was dreaming, you woke me up now I'll never know the end of my story.* I want nothing more than for my dream to have a sweet ending but nothing is guaranteed. Liza asked, *was it about Marvin?* No, *it was about my husband and I, we were back together again and things were wonderful.* Liz, you said the right thing, *was,* you know I never tell you what to do but you should cut your losses with that one.

*Really Liza! I would never have
expected you to be that cold.*

*Liz I'm tired of seeing you sad,
unhappy, I'm used to the Liz who just left
Miami, when can I have my friend back?*

*I Love him Liza and that's that! Liza
let's get our luggage, grab a drink and find
the car.*

Since returning from Miami, I thought often of an
actual reconciliation especially after that dream
I had, but the belief residing in my mind was that
I had-had enough of the distrust and abuse. I'll
love Able forever; however, my life has been much
better with him gone. In my indiscretions I found
a friend, Marvin proved to be quite the young man.
He restored my confidences. I had begun to view
myself as an inanimate object instead of human
being. I viewed my beauty, intelligence, and power
as limited, living with Able's addiction on my
shoulders. Marvin helped me find my voice again.
Fifteen hundred miles away this man painted a
vivid picture of what I was dealing with. Marvin
had watched his biological mother worry herself
into an early grave. His younger brother uses
heroin, while his sister's drug of choice is crack
cocaine the same drug my husband uses. He opened
up his life story to help me see that no matter
how much I want his addiction to go away it's his
problem to fix. I was comfortable sharing my chaos
with Marvin. Opening up with him was the start to
more secrets being unlocked? Marvin inspired me.

Fondness

I remember you most for your humor'
How you conjure up uncontrollable roars of
Laugher

How you put a bug in my ear
And it's tune made me smile
As tears of joy turned into
Laughter
How you listened to my every word
Recalling back my dreams and fears
Acknowledging my struggles
By nodding your head causing great
Laughter
To bubble forth in the midst of dread

Remembering your soft touch
Without permission that made me
Laugh
Just because the nerve of you

How you gave me hope
When I was in despair

How you held my hand
Showing me that you really care
How you read my body
From top to bottom
And oh yeah
From back to front

How you placed me in admiration
Of your wonderful nature
How you walked with me
If just for a little while
Calming my fears igniting my smile
O yeah and the uncontrollable
Laughter

I will never forget you
No matter the distance
You are my friend
The one I remember
When things are bad I will call on you
When times are good I'll need you too
When things are left to chance
I will remember our romance
Oh yeah and the uncontrollable
Laughter

Chapter 28

For the past several months I only shared the ugly details of my dependency with my counselor, because I felt everyone else would judge and treat both Able and myself differently. During our courtship, and soon thereafter we formed many friendships with other couples who knew nothing of his drug addiction. To them Able and I were perfect. All the couples admired our bond. I felt compromised every time we were not being our authentic selves. It has taken me a long time to get to where I am today. I am finally ready to let go of both our addictions. I am a strong woman of modest faith, making baby steps all the way to my sobriety. I'm not sure how long it will take me to forgive myself for being a participant in enabling Cain and forsaking Able, but the first step, I'm taking now.

June 7, 2010
My One True Love

My dearest Able I am writing this letter to say goodbye with tears blinding the page and snot draining from my nostrils because it's over and I know it, even if you won't admit it. I've dreamed of someone calling me with the devastating news and my heart felt like it was about to jump out of my body, so I've decided to stop tormenting myself. Nothing I do has ever been to your satisfaction except love making and you don't need that from me anymore. Our time together has seen its last curtain call and the auditorium is empty. There is no one front and center to throw stones anymore. The streets, Lauren, and your family have won. My weary frame has nothing left to offer; if I stick around any longer my children will be motherless. I have been assaulted in the worst possible way by the man who professed to love me more than anything; however, there is something and someone you love more and I can't stand the hurt anymore. I honestly have never loved any man as much as I have loved you, but love means nothing to you because you have never learned how to appreciate your own worth. Able, I want and pray that your future be filled with real joy; I have only the best wishes for your recovery. Deep down your hidden torment has become my visible plight, and now that it has taken its toll on me I have no choice but to let go. Maybe there is a better place for us both. Maybe we needed this one last performance together so that this two decade love affair could be exposed for what it has turned out to be a teenage infatuation that was never meant to be anything more. I know that I am still, but whether or not you are still, shall remain this big open space. I know you loved me as best you could from within your definition; however, love has never been enough for our imperfect minds, we always want more, need more, and desire plenty. Speaking only for myself true love is all I have ever wanted, needed, or desired from you but somewhere down the line we lost respectability for each other, and that is never good in a young marriage. We lost the only thing that would keep us together and that is our love

176

for God, because without his guidance and strength we are doomed not only as a couple but as individuals. Our chances went from ninety-ninety point nine percent to zero quickly. We allowed a place for Satan and this is what he has reduced us to, at least me. I am writing my only true love a goodbye letter because my heart and stomach are no longer strong enough for the blows. You told me just the other day that I'm second to none that's funny, because I feel like I'm beneath your foot. No one who ever professed to love me as you have has ever placed me in a position where I feel unworthy of admiration. You have grown tired of your existence and I can't heal your broken spirit. You living with your child in the same household as Lauren won't heal your disease but I'm out of my knowledge base, so all I can do now is pray. I wish you a brighter tomorrow, and maybe somewhere down the line we will be able to forgive ourselves for messing up our friendship. I love you Able, but I have to say goodbye, because death is not an option for me.

Book Club Notes

Me Again

The smile that **restores**
Sight of the visually impaired
The vocals that **revive**
Comatose dreams
The hips that **recover**
From childbirth pain
The harmonious drums that **Replace**
Sirens transporting the Afflicted
The fresh aromas of summers **return**
Unpolluted by the scent of death
The naturalness of my **renewed**
Roots **recreating**
Me Again
Here I am beautiful me
Reciting those lines of poetry
Recounting those past mistakes
Reclaiming power over my mental State
Rejuvenated by that womanly spirit
Residing in me at his will
Redeeming myself from sins appeal
Rebuking my wrongs
Reconciling my heart to do right
Receiving his forgiveness
Rejoicing in my victories
To
Reason with Stability
Here I am
Me Again

179

Made in the USA
Charleston, SC
27 June 2011